What on earth had her father been thinking about, Alex wondered vexedly, consigning her little brother Ben to the guardianship of his friend Professor Nicholas Devlin? It was bad enough to have to go out to Bangkok where Professor Devlin lived—but then Alex realised that she had no guarantee that he would allow her to stay on there with her brother . . .

AUTUMN IN BANGKOK

BY

JACQUELINE GILBERT

MILLS & BOON LIMITED

15–16 BROOK'S MEWS
LONDON W1A 1DR

First published 1980

Australian copyright 1981
Philippine copyright 1981
This edition 1981

© Jacqueline Gilbert 1980

ISBN 0 263 73412 9

Set in Monophoto Baskerville 10 on 11½ pt.

Made and printed in Great Britain by
Richard Clay (The Chaucer Press), Ltd., Bungay, Suffolk

For
ANTHONY
with thanks

CHAPTER ONE

'MR HICKS will see you now, Miss Templar.'

The clerk stood by the door and directed his remark at the young girl sitting in the reception area. At his words Alexandra Templar looked up, honey-blonde hair falling back to reveal a rather pale, withdrawn face which was transformed into one of serene beauty by the smile that followed. She rose quickly to her feet and crossed the floor with unconcealed eagerness.

The clerk closed the door behind her feeling as though he had been handed a gift by that smile. There was a faint, lingering hint of perfume in the air and as he returned to his desk he bemoaned silently to himself that such a smasher should be wasted on Old Man Hicks.

Old Man Hicks would have argued the point. He was fully able to appreciate Alex Templar, having two perfectly adequate eyes in his head. While he would not have gone so far as to call her a 'smasher'—such an expression being outside his vocabulary—she was, to his mind, a very lovely girl.

James Hicks had watched Alex grow from a quiet, over-serious child into a calm, capable young woman of twenty-two, although he was just beginning to find out that behind that cool demeanour lay fires that had, hitherto, been banked down. Being an elderly bachelor James did not have first-hand knowledge of children, but it had always seemed to him that Alex had had to grow up too quickly. Her mother had died immediately after the birth of a second child, a son, when

Alex was fourteen. Her father, Charles Templar, had employed a succession of nannies and housekeepers, but it was Alex who had taken the sickly baby to her heart with a fiercely protective instinct surprising in one so young.

In James' opinion the girl had missed out on a normal adolescence and while Charles Templar was a brilliant academic and noted archaeologist he had never been much of a father to either Alex or to her brother, Ben.

Charles Templar was now dead. Unexpectedly, at the age of sixty, while collating material for his latest book, on the island of Singapore. His will, a new one made only six months ago without James' knowledge, was the cause of the anxious look on Alex's face as she entered his office and James rose to his feet with as much agility as his sixty-two years allowed and held out his hand.

'Alex, my dear girl, how are you? You're looking extremely well, if I may be so bold. And Ben? Still doing well at school?'

Alex allowed herself to be placed in a chair and humoured him for a few minutes, talking about Ben and school, his health and her own job in the library, but at last she could stand it no longer.

'Have you had a reply, Mr Hicks?'

Her words checked the benign expression on James's face and recalled business to hand and the unpleasant news he had to impart.

'Yes, indeed—now, let me see . . .' and he reached for a folder placed in readiness on his desk and opened it.

'From Professor Devlin himself?' Alex prompted, and James peered over his spectacles.

'No. I've never been in direct contact with the Professor. All correspondence has been conducted through his own solicitors in Bangkok.' He paused and pursed his lips before saying gently: 'I'm afraid Ben will have to go, my dear.' He saw the colour come and go in her cheeks and rushed on: 'There's nothing we can do about it, Alex, and who can tell, this might be a wonderful opportunity for him . . .'

'We can't be certain, though,' protested Alex, her voice distressed. 'Oh, I know you're only trying to make things easier for me, Mr Hicks, but all my instincts tell me it's wrong. Eight is so young to be uprooted and thrust among strangers—in a foreign country too! Especially now, when there's just the two of us left. Father never had much time for either of us, but he did mean a certain amount of security just by existing. Now he's gone Ben is vulnerable, and this guardian we've never met and know nothing about is taking away the only secure things left—home, school and me!'

'The Professor has indicated his consent that you . . .'

'Did you explain the awful time we had with Ben when he was a baby and the operations, and how he nearly died? Did you tell Professor Devlin that Ben's just beginning to lead a more normal life? Does he . . .'

'I explained the situation fully, as we planned the last time you came to the office, Alex, but I did warn you then that Professor Devlin is quite within his rights to send for Ben, didn't I? I cautioned you not to expect too much, so that the disappointment wouldn't be so severe.' James Hicks's voice was quiet but firm, and Alex nodded, biting her lip and blinking rapidly to stop the unshed tears from falling. 'Professor Devlin's solicitors have contacted the hospital on his behalf for a report on Ben which appears to be most encouraging, which does show a degree of concern over Ben's welfare,' James went on. 'As you know, by the terms of your father's will he is Ben's legal guardian until the boy comes of age at eighteen. After that he has control of Ben's finances until his twenty-first birthday . . .'

'And mine till I'm twenty-five,' put in Alex bitterly. 'It's positively Victorian!'

James continued, ignoring her interjection: 'For some men, our suggestion that Ben remains in England to continue his schooling and live in your care would have been an easy way out to taking an unknown boy into his household. Professor Devlin doesn't wish to shirk his responsibilities,' and he regarded her gravely.

'Why Father couldn't have left us as we are, I don't know,' Alex burst out resentfully. 'It's suited him perfectly well up to now while he's been hunting ruined temples and prehistoric remains all over the place!' She broke off and stared miserably out of the window. The normal, busy street scene met her eyes and irrationally it offended her. When her own life was about to be splintered and jettisoned, Norwich had no business to be so predictable.

James took advantage of the break in the passionate flow of words to say cajolingly:

'Try and take a more positive approach to the matter, Alex, if you can, my dear. I've found, over the years, that it's absolutely useless wasting time and energy on the whys and wherefores. We shall never know what was in your father's mind when he made his will. We must accept that Ben is to go to Bangkok to live in the care of his guardian. Professor Devlin has repeated his invitation for you to travel with your brother, and has again extended the wish that you stay until such time as you feel . . .'

'We know nothing about this Nicholas Devlin person,' complained Alex, 'except that he's a Professor at . . .'

'Chulalongkorn University, Bangkok,' provided James helpfully as she floundered, and Alex continued dismissively:

'Yes, that's right . . . he's an anthropologist and knew my father when they were at Cambridge together . . . and that's *all* we know. Mr Hicks, why should an elderly professor want to land himself with an energetic boy of eight he's never met? Is it money, do you think . . .?'

James gave a shocked exclamation and leaned earnestly forward. 'My dear Alex, I beg you to restrain yourself. Your father naturally made provision, but in no way could it constitute a reason. Professor Devlin is the author of many books, all critically acclaimed, so I'm told, and is held in as high repute in his own field as your father is in his. I must advise you, Alex, not to let your disappointment lead you into rash statements. I can only suggest that you go to Thailand with Ben, meet the Professor, and help him change his mind.'
James was sincere in his advice but secretly held out little hope. He rather thought that Charles Templar had passed on to his colleague his own dismissive feelings towards his daughter. In James's opinion the man should never have married. He had little interest in his firstborn and when he finally had a son, it was a puny, weak thing, with little chance of survival, and it cost him the life of his wife. The tragedy, instead of drawing him closer to his daughter and home had pushed him further away and his work and ambition took over his life. A strange man, Charles Templar, thought James. A man happier digging in the past than living

in the present. He looked at the pale, frowning face in front of him and felt anger. Wearing a tweed suit of russet brown with a gold silk scarf at her neck, Alex had brought a touch of autumn into his sombre office. It gave him pleasure to look at her and he only wished he had had happier news for her this September afternoon. He said gently:

'It will be much better for you to accept the situation, Alex, with good grace. Better for yourself and ultimately better for Ben.' It was his trump card. There was silence for a long moment and then Alex took a deep breath and nodded decisively.

'Yes, you're right, Mr Hicks. Goodness, what should we have done without you all these years?' Her face went pensive as she looked out of the window. 'I shall miss autumn . . . my favourite season.' A pause and she gave him a determined smile. 'Ah, well, we shall spend autumn in Bangkok. Right. When do we go?'

The monsoon wind, sweeping in off the Indian Ocean and covering Singapore Island with an impenetrable blanket of torrential rain, seemed to renew its efforts to outdo the performance on stage at the large and impressive National Theatre.

An unusually loud burst of the elements coincided with the last strains of music, made more apparent by the open-air structure of the building. To Alex, sitting at the back of the highly raked auditorium, the weather was only part of a myriad of unusual sights and sounds she had been experiencing since her arrival with Ben on the Island that day. She had been persuaded to 'go off and enjoy yourself' by a friendly Australian family who had travelled from London on the same plane. They were in the next room to the

Templar brother and sister in the hotel and Alex had no qualms about leaving Ben under their protection, especially as they had a son of a similar age. Finding that the National Theatre was having a visit from a Russian ballet company and that evening they were performing the ballet *Giselle*, Alex needed no further prompting. As for the rain—that was no deterrent to a hardy English girl!

As the applause finally died down Alex began to collect her things together, aware of the interest she was affording. Her long fair hair and pale skin was such a contrast to those around her and feeling rather shy she busied herself with putting on her raincoat, still wet from the journey to the theatre. Everything was damp, even the atmosphere, which was warm and humid.

Alex grinned to herself at the picture she must present—flat, sensible sandals and raincoat were not what she would have chosen under normal conditions for an evening out at the theatre! On such a night, however, anything else would have been totally impractical, for she couldn't get a taxi and had had to walk from the hotel, with the aid of a street map, through the rain and ever deepening puddles.

As she waited her turn to move out of the row and into the gangway she swept her eyes round the building for a last look at the architecture. With three open sides exposed to the elements it seemed more like a stadium than a theatre, and at the moment rain was pouring off the roof and cascading relentlessly to the ground like a miniature Niagara Falls! Capable of holding well over three thousand people, the weather keeping many away, it was barely half full.

Alex's row began to move out now, and she concentrated finding a firm footing on the flight of steps leading down to the exit gangway. During another halt her attention was held by the sight of an attractive European woman who was making her way up from the expensive seats at the front of the auditorium.

She hadn't had to walk through puddles to get here tonight, thought Alex with some amusement, taking in the chic black dress, high-heeled shoes and well-groomed hair-style! Alex wondered what nationality the woman was and felt a wave of homesickness sweep over her. She was suddenly aware of her own loneliness and vulnerability and hoped she would be able to be lucky enough to find a taxi, now eager to return to the hotel and Ben.

Perhaps this eagerness made her a little inattentive to her feet and she stumbled slightly on the last step, reaching out automatically to save herself from over-balancing. She was held and steadied and smiled her thanks as she found firm footing.

Surprisingly she received no smile in return, the face that looked down at her was quite stern, and giving a rather curt nod the man moved on, and Alex realised that he was in the group of Singaporeans that included the European woman. Lucky her, to have such an escort! Big, broad and strong were Alex's first fleeting impressions, followed by more definite attributes—light, penetrating grey eyes, a craggy face deeply tanned and thick brown hair, and evening clothes worn with ease.

Oh, yes, the stuff dreams were made of, chuckled Alex, seeing the back of his head and shoulders disappearing out into the darkness, but he was soon forgotten when it became apparent that there were no taxis to be had.

Only now did Alex eye the weather worriedly. It began to dawn on even her inexperienced eyes that this was something more than a normal monsoon, but the unconcern on the faces of the Singaporeans leaving the theatre as they laughingly put up their brightly coloured umbrellas slightly dispelled her fears. Walking along the raised platforms lining the pavements, conscious of the deep gutters gushing with fast, overflowing water, Alex thought that if they weren't worried, why should she be?

Clemenceau Avenue. Alex fumbled in her pocket for the street map and crossly found that she had lost it. She peered up again at the street sign and then at her surroundings. Yes, she was on the right road, and although she pulled her raincoat more closely to her it was merely a reflex action for she was wet through to the skin already.

Refusing to be alarmed by the fact that there were few vehicles on the road and those that were moved slowly, their headlights showing that the road was awash with water now, Alex hurried on.

She had been able, up to this point, in keeping her thoughts free of Professor Devlin, waiting for them in Bangkok. Now he flew unbidden to her mind and she gave an inward groan, and then just as quickly her own self-assurance stiffened. It was nothing to the Professor if she had decided to come to Singapore first, to see her father's grave, nothing to do with him at all! And if he thought he could boss her around then he was in for a surprise!

These rebellious words cheered her up until Alex realised that she was lost. Somehow nothing looked familiar. This part of the road was ill-lit and nearly deserted. A car was coming slowly towards her, its headlights blurred through the rain, water spraying up from the wheels. On the other side of the road she could make out a faint light, probably one of the many

tiny eating places that abound in Singapore. There she
would ask the way.

Head down against the driving wind and rain, she
splashed through water which now swirled round her
feet. Nearly half-way across the wide road she heard a
shout behind her. Startled, she swung round, eyes
half-closed, hair whipping across her face, to find that
the car had stopped and the driver was running towards her.

All warnings of girls out on their own in a foreign
city rushed to her and she turned and ran, ploughing
through the water with staggering, uneven strides. She
heaved for breath, the blood pounding in her ears and
an inner voice repeating over and over again—how
stupid, how stupid—until an arm was flung round her
waist and she was brought to her knees.

There was a short, humiliating struggle, throughout
which she clung relentlessly to her handbag, and then
she was hauled, gasping and sobbing, to her feet.

'Enough! That's enough, do you hear?' The hands
that gripped her shoulders shook her hard to give
emphasis to the order. 'Stop fighting, you little fool,
and listen to me!'

The words finally penetrated Alex's frightened
senses. Amazingly they were words she could understand—her assailant was speaking in English! The
fight went out of her. She peered upwards, the rain
hitting her face and the wind flapping her coat, and
nearly collapsed in amazement. Looking as big a mess
as she did, with brows drawn together, chest heaving
as he tried to control his breathing, the man from the
theatre glared down at her.

'Damn it all, girl, what the hell are you playing at?
Are you tired of life?' he snarled, nostrils flaring as
anger flowed from him in no uncertain manner. As she

stared in bewilderment at his vehemence he thrust her round, muttering an oath, his hands digging into the soft flesh of her upper arms with agonising force. 'See that?' he demanded, indicating the murky distance between where they were standing and the light she was making for. 'Three yards away from here is an extremely deep and at this particular moment, dangerous, monsoon drain!'

With quickening heart-beat Alex looked up and searched his face, seeing beneath the anger an awareness of a man who had just gone through a bad few minutes. Almost fearfully she turned her head and by concentrating hard could make out that the flood water ahead was moving much more rapidly and with a frightening turbulence.

'Let's get out of here.' Her rescuer half dragged, half carried her back to his car which was as he had left it, door wide open, engine still running and the headlights blazing. He led her round to the passenger side and helped her in, joining her a few seconds later with the words: 'The water's rising—if we're not careful we'll be stranded like those poor devils,' and he gestured to what she hadn't noticed before, cars ahead, obviously abandoned.

For a few moments all was silence as he backed up slowly and turned into a side street, murmuring for her information:

'This is a dual carriageway, with the drain down the centre, so I can't drive back the way I came. Now then, which is your hotel?' and when Alex told him he gave a rasping laugh. 'My God, I might have guessed you'd be going in the wrong direction! Well, getting you there, Naiad, is completely out of the question. I know from personal experience that Orchard Road is under water and cut off. Is there anywhere else I can take you? Have you friends on the Island who can put you up?'

'No,' muttered Alex, thinking the man had a twisted sense of humour calling her Naiad. She didn't feel like a water nymph at all, more like a drowned rat! She stirred restlessly. 'I'm making a terrible mess of your car,' she said miserably.

'That makes two of us,' came the short rejoinder. He gave a heavy sigh and said roughly: 'Then you'd better come with me,' and engaging gear he set off with no further words between them, both staring through the windscreen, wipers barely able to take the downpour, concentrating on the flooded road ahead.

To Alex the whole thing was like a bad dream. Even now she could hardly comprehend the danger she had been in. She thought fleetingly of Ben, wondering if she would be able to get some word to the Australian couple, who must be worrying by now. More reluctantly she thought of the man by her side.

She sneaked him a glance, her heart sinking. If she looked a wreck he didn't look much better. Wrestling with her in the flood water had played havoc with his evening suit. The thick hair was now plastered to his head, rivulets of water continually running down his face and dripping on to the once immaculate white shirt. The black bow tie hung limp and half undone, and if it wasn't so awful it would be excruciatingly funny, thought Alex in despair. He had every right to be angry with her . . . and where was his lady-friend? He had obviously dropped her off somewhere. It was as obvious he knew his way on the Island and by a series of roundabout routes they at last slowed down outside a modern skyscraper hotel. The car keys were handed over to a waiting doorman and when Alex protested feebly to entering the brightly lit foyer her escort said dryly:

'You'll find you're not the only one to be water-logged,' and propelled her through the swing doors. 'Wait here while I get my key.'

He's used to giving orders, thought Alex, too weary and thankful to feel resentment. And he was quite right. The foyer was full of people, in varying degrees of distress, all discoursing loudly on their personal predicaments. After having a brief talk with the desk clerk her large friend came back and hustled her into one of the lifts and they eventually emerged on the fourteenth floor.

Trailing him, Alex had to admire the way he carried off their appearance, simply by ignoring it. He had passed the time of day with a couple in the lift and now walked with casual ease along the thick-carpeted corridor in very much the same manner he must have left it some hours earlier.

He finally stopped outside a door, unlocked it and went in, leaving the door open for Alex to follow. She stood in the doorway and watched him switch on a couple of table lamps, pull the curtains and then turn to look at her.

'Come in, I won't eat you.' The tone was dry. He began to empty his pockets of wallet, key-ring and sundry items, placing them carefully on to a small table set in the middle of the room.

'I've already been a terrible nuisance to you. Wouldn't it be easier if I took a room in the hotel for tonight—and then you can forget all about me?' She tried to sound coolly competent, but feared she didn't succeed. A handful of coins were dropped on to the table before he straightened.

'I agree, Naiad, much easier. Unfortunately there isn't a room to be had,' and seeing her unbelieving

face, he added patiently: 'I enquired at the desk when
we came in. The floods have disrupted everything,
including the airport. All the hotels, not only this one,
are in chaos with tourists who should have left but
can't battling with new arrivals who managed to get
through. Despite its size this one is full to bursting.
You can, of course, join others in similar circumstances to yourself in the lounges or restaurant, where
I understand emergency services are being set up.
Otherwise you're stuck with me.' He paused. 'Well?'
and then, almost before she could reply his wrist came
up to take a quick look at the time. 'Let's clear the air
on everything, shall we? It's gone midnight and I'm
flying out early tomorrow, so there's not much left of
the night now anyway.' He crossed the room and shut
the door behind her, his voice wearily amused. 'I shall
use the couch and you the bed. Don't be worrying
about your virtue, Naiad. At this particular moment
I'm far more interested in a hot bath, dry clothes and a
stiff drink, in that order, and there's a lock on the door
if you're still not sure.' He left her and walked into the
bedroom and she heard the sound of drawers being
opened. On his return, a few seconds later, he was
carrying some articles of clothing. He opened the remaining door off, saying: 'This is the bathroom and
I'll be the perfect gentleman and let you use it. I shall
beg the use of another further down the corridor.
You'll find soap and towels in there. Dry clothing is
more of a problem, but you'll have to make do with
what I've got.' He threw the bundle to her. 'Leave
your own clothes outside the door and I'll get room
service to collect them.' His mouth twisted into a derisive smile. 'Try not to drown yourself for the second
time tonight, Naiad,' and he bowed her into the bathroom.

It was a relief to be told what to do. Alex gave an uncertain smile and did as she was bidden.

Emerging later, pink and scrubbed and feeling marvellously clean, she found her host sitting relaxed in one of the two armchairs, a glass in his hand and casual shirt and trousers replacing the ill-fated theatre garb. He lifted his head as she entered and drawled:

'I was beginning to think it might be necessary to do another rescue job.'

'I had to wash my hair too,' Alex explained, hovering uncertainly and tying the belt of his enormous silk dressing gown more tightly round her neat waist.

She had washed through her wispy underwear and it had dried while she was bathing and the robe was perfectly adequate a coverage, but perhaps it accentuated her shape too much for comfort, and as his eyes flicked her up and down the colour in her cheeks deepened slightly.

'So I see. There is, Naiad, a general improvement,' he observed dryly, and then: 'Is there someone you can telephone, to let them know you're safe? Won't there be someone worrying about you?' His glance went to her ringless hand. 'Not a husband, I see, but a relation? Surely you're not on the Island alone?' His voice was accusingly abrupt.

'A brother,' said Alex quickly, knowing he didn't mean an eight-year-old little boy who, she hoped, was fast asleep in his bed. Her host nodded and rising to his feet crossed to the bedroom door and pushed it open.

'The switchboard will get your hotel number,' he told her, indicating the telephone by the bed. Murmuring her thanks, Alex slipped barefooted by him, and he shut the door behind her.

She got through to her hotel and spoke to the Australian couple who were just becoming alarmed by the reports on their television screen. Ben was asleep, they told her, and Alex said she would get in touch with them again in the morning when the conditions could be better assessed. Feeling happier for the contact, she returned to the sitting room and tried to thank her host, firstly for the use of the telephone and then for his part in the evening's escapade, but he wouldn't let her finish, breaking in brusquely with:

'Well? Was he worried, this brother of yours?'

Alex thrust her hands in the pockets of the robe and raised her chin, replying with a degree of defensiveness:

'Naturally. Wouldn't anyone be?'

'So one would suppose,' he granted, a hint of sarcasm still in his voice. 'What the devil does he think he's doing, letting you out alone like this? It's a fool thing on any night, but on this one extremely dangerous.'

'Oh, really, I'm perfectly capable of going to the theatre on my own . . .' began Alex.

'And perfectly capable of drowning in twelve feet of monsoon drain,' he suggested, with insulting affability.

Alex stared at him in dismay, digesting this bit of information. 'Twelve feet?' she echoed slowly, her imagination running riot.

'Give or take. And about eighteen feet wide. With sloping concrete sides making it difficult to climb out,' he went on remorselessly, 'and a strong current full of the usual debris . . . bits of wood, tree branches, vegetation, a rat and a snake or two.' Alex winced and he nodded to the television set placed in the corner. 'I've just been watching some news flashes. There's been four deaths in similar circumstances already.'

.Subdued, Alex said: 'You've made your point.'

'I sincerely hope so.'

Alex felt like a naughty pupil being given a ticking
off by the headmaster.

'Look, I've said thank you ... I know it's totally
inadequate for what you've done, and I'm sorry I've
ruined your evening. I promise I won't go out alone
again.'

'I take it you're new to the Island?'

She padded over to the other chair and tucked herself into it and nodded. 'We only arrived today. This
rain is unusual, surely? I mean, I've read about tropical rainfall and monsoons, but this seems excessive.'

His smile was a grim one. 'Yes, indeed. The weather
pundits are declaring the highest rainfall recorded in
Island history even now. Goodness knows what it will
reach if things go on as they are. Do you think your
arrival on these shores is significant, Naiad?' and the
cool grey eyes teased. 'The furies seem to be outdoing
even themselves. Have you offended them in any
way?'

Alex hugged her knees and, her library background
coming to her aid, quoted smilingly: ' "Now the great
winds shoreward blow, now the salt tides seaward
flow." '

'Mm ... *The Forsaken Merman*. Rather apt for a
water nymph.' He indicated a plate of sandwiches and
a tray of coffee things. 'Do Naiads get hungry?' he
asked quizzically, and Alex grinned.

'This Naiad does. Thanks, I'm famished. I was
hoping they weren't there for show,' and she was rewarded by a smile of amusement. There was silence
while she munched on the sandwiches and drank the
coffee. Her host lit a narrow cigar and refilled his
glass, and out of his line of vision she studied him

thoughtfully. He was a big man, well over six feet, with a breadth of shoulder that denoted physical strength. His skin was tanned as though he spent a great deal of time in the sun and although he wasn't handsome there was attractiveness in his features, especially when he smiled. His manner was authoritative, which in the circumstances of their meeting was natural, but she had seen a glimpse of kindness and humour. She found his eyes upon her and said quickly:

'Your voice has been puzzling me all evening. I've been trying to place your accent. Are you English?'

'God forbid,' he replied calmly, sitting again and relaxing back against the cushions watching the cigar smoke rise thinly into the air. 'I'm American-Irish and you'll not accuse me of being English, Naiad.'

'Well, I'm sorry if you think I've insulted you,' she came back laughing.

'If you know your history no true-blooded Irishman would ever take kindly to the thought.' He studied the liquid in his glass. 'I was born in Ireland and have our patron saint's name to prove it,' and he took a drink, adding wryly: 'And this whisky isn't a patch on our own malt brew.'

American-Irish. So that was it, the slight Western drawl with the Irish lilt, neither accent pronounced but both countries contributing a flavour to his voice making it distinctive. She wondered how old he was. Difficult to guess. Probably mid-thirties. And his name was Patrick. Again his regard broke into her thoughts and she felt forced to speak.

'Perhaps it's as well you didn't know *I* was English,' she joked, 'or else you might have helped me in tonight.'

He replied placidly: 'Oh, I knew you were English.'

She stared in surprise. 'How did you know that?'
and he smiled his slow, almost mocking smile.

'I guessed the minute I set eyes on you in the
theatre. A haughty English Miss, I thought, as cool as
a cucumber, looking as though she ought to have a
parasol and be drinking tea on the Vicarage lawn.'

Alex felt nonplussed and smiled uncertainly. He
rose unhurriedly to his feet, placing his empty glass on
the table.

'You seem to be having difficulty keeping your eyes
open. I've a phone call to make and then you can go to
bed.'

Alex allowed the yawn she had been struggling with
win and said ruefully: 'I'm sorry, but it's been rather a
tiring day. Er . . . shall I use the bathroom first?'

He paused by the bedroom door and replied
gravely: 'Yes, perhaps you'd better.'

While chewing on some of her host's toothpaste
Alex thought over what he had just said about her.
Haughty English Miss! She lifted her head and gazed
seriously at herself in the mirror. Haughty? She knew
that when she was unsure of herself she tended to
withdraw behind a barrier of coolness. She had been
accused more than once of being an ice-maiden, but it
wasn't true. At least, she supposed it wasn't—hoped it
wasn't. That was one of the accusations Richard had
hurled at her, but she knew it was only a get-out for
him. For a while she had thought her heart broken,
but it wasn't. Richard's going had not altered the fact
that whoever took her on took Ben too.

She splashed water on her face and dried off. Naiad.
She smiled into the mirror, wide blue eyes smiling
back. She liked the way he called her Naiad. His voice
was . . . interesting. Stop daydreaming, Alex, she told
herself sternly, dousing the light. Her large friend was

carrying a couple of blankets from the bedroom as she re-entered and throwing them down on the couch, he said:

'I've organised with room service to have your clothes brought up here first thing tomorrow.'

'Thank you.' Alex took breath. 'Look, I suppose there's no use suggesting that I take the couch? I mean, I'd fit it so much better than you—you're so large.' Her voice wavered beneath the amusement on his face.

'Don't deny me the chance of another chivalrous act, Naiad, there's a good girl. I shall stay as I am and the couch will do very well for what remains of the night.' He put a hand under her chin and tilted her head. 'I've just realised who you remind me of. Put a band round your hair and you'd make a grand Alice in Wonderland.'

Perhaps, in the circumstances, it was as well she reminded him of a child. Subconsciously she fell back on her haughty English Miss look.

'I'm very grateful for all you've done. I'll never be able to repay you . . .'

'Not another word.' He stared down at her, one brow raised quizzically. 'I'll take my own payment.' Before she knew what he intended his mouth came down on hers. 'Mm, nice and tasty, Naiad.'

That damned toothpaste!

'Goodnight. We'll see what tomorrow brings. We'll get you back to your brother some way.'

'Yes. Thank you . . . goodnight,' and Alex, colour high, escaped to the bedroom.

When she woke the next morning her watch said six o'clock. For a moment she couldn't place where she was and then it all came back. Throwing off the covers, she tiptoed to the window and pulled the blind. The morning was grey but dry. From her high perch she could see that traffic was moving down below in the street and in the distance an aircraft was coming in to land. So the airport was open again. Good. She hadn't relished the thought of sending the Professor a telegram saying they would be delayed. That would have meant going into explanations and the less the worthy Professor knew about this little lot the better. It was her aim to show him how capable she was, not to prove otherwise. He probably wouldn't be too keen on the idea of her spending the night in a stranger's bed either. For the first time it struck her that there were some people who would not be able to believe that she had spent it alone.

She abandoned the window, knowing there was no time to waste. Opening the door slowly, she saw that the room beyond was empty, sounds of the shower coming from the bathroom. She saw her own dress and coat lying across a chair, clean and pressed, and she soft-footed over and gathered them up, hurrying back into the bedroom. She dressed quickly and found paper and pencil, writing hastily in her neat, round hand:

'Dear Patrick, In the cool, clear light of day it's difficult to imagine last night, but it did happen and if it hadn't been for you I might not be around now! I know you don't want thanks, but you'll have to take sincere ones from me for all you've done. If you know your Longfellow, and I'm sure you do, then "Ships that pass in the night" fits. Yours most gratefully, Naiad . . . or rather—Alexandra Jane Templar, Norwich, England.'

She propped the note on the top of a suitcase already waiting by the door and with one last look to see that she hadn't forgotten anything, let herself quietly out of the room.

CHAPTER TWO

THE Captain of Thai International flight Singapore to Bangkok announced politely that they would be landing at Bangkok Airport in just under the hour.

Alex caught Ben's excited look and wished she felt as bright and happy as he did. Less than five hours' sleep plus the fact that the plane was taking them nearer and nearer the unknown Professor Devlin were reasons enough to account for a thumping great headache just beginning to show its presence.

She closed her eyes, her thoughts returning to their visit that morning to St Andrew's Cathedral with its beautiful white spires and Gothic architecture. Surrounded by the busy city, the Cathedral stood undisturbed, the grass and tall trees giving a very English feeling to the scene. In some measure going there had been a kind of pilgrimage, a laying of her father's memory and a hope for a lessening of the bitterness inside her. What she did find was pity for all he had missed—surely her father had ended up a lonely man?

On the journey by bus from the city to the airport they had seen signs of the havoc the previous forty-eight hours had wrought and passing one of the large monsoon drains Alex was made aware the extent of her danger. Innocuous-looking now that the flood water had receded, the steep sides were covered in mud and slime and as her imagination began to take over a shiver of revulsion went down her spine.

Yes, Singapore was a place to be remembered, and if some things lingered in the memory longer than others she was able to persuade herself that day-dreaming hurt no one, in small doses.

She suddenly wished that she had waited, to thank her rescuer in person rather than leaving a note, but it had been the sensible thing to do. Go out of his life as quickly as she had entered it. Yes, she would re-member Singapore.

A bustle at the other end of the plane heralded the arrival of the Thai hostesses come to clear the food trays. In their purple uniforms of Oriental-style tops and slim long skirts they moved gracefully down the gangways. With their dark hair and magnolia skins the two smiling girls made Alex very much aware of Eas-tern beauty.

'What time do we get in?' Ben asked, and Alex re-plied:

'Five-thirtyish, I think,' and when he returned his attention to the map of their route spread out before him, she studied him, a sudden surge of emotion sweeping over her, as quickly suppressed. Emotion clouded the judgment. It was not emotion but prac-ticalities on which she was going to plead their case with Professor Devlin.

Ben was slight for an eight-year-old and rather frail-looking. A premature birth and numerous stays in hos-pital were to blame. He too had blue eyes and blond hair, almost white, and his nature was sunny and placid with a tendency towards being a bookworm, al-though he enjoyed swimming and was beginning to participate in certain games that were not too taxing.

The calm voice of their hostess announced that they would be landing in fifteen minutes and would passen-gers kindly check that their seat belts were in position.

'Nearly there,' Ben said eagerly. 'I wonder what Professor Devlin will be like, Alex?'

'Oh, a mixture of all Father's friends rolled into one, I should think,' replied Alex brightly. 'He must be nice, though, or else Father wouldn't have chosen him to look after us.'

This answer satisfied Ben as Alex intended. Academically this Devlin person could be brilliant, but as a human being she wasn't prepared to take a bet. So far as Ben was concerned, she was keeping her anxiety to herself.

'If it's half-past five then that means it's ten-thirty in the morning back home. There's seven hours' difference in time, you see, Alex. Our geography teacher spent one whole lesson on Thailand when he knew I was going. Thailand means Land of the Free, did you know that, Alex?'

Alex shook her head. Land of the Free! Was anyone ever free? she wondered cynically.

Ben tugged her sleeve. 'Look, we're coming lower— see the canals? They're called klongs.'

'Are they? It's very flat—looks as though there's been flooding here too.'

Ben nodded. 'We're going at the best time. The rains are finishing and the cool is just beginning.'

'Cool?' Alex raised her brows and laughed. 'I think their cool will be like a good English summer!'

The DC10 began to lose height rapidly and then the airport lay ahead of them, runways stretching out invitingly. A rapid impression of wooden houses on stilts, palm trees, shining water and bright sunshine and they were down.

Formalities of arrival went smoothly and in the arrival lounge brother and sister stopped, uncertain. Everyone else seemed involved in being met or were moving towards the exits in a purposeful manner.

'What happens now?' Ben asked, staring round.

'Alex, do you see? They don't shake hands like we do, they sort of make a bow and pray with their hands.'

'It's called making a *wai*. You aren't the only one who's done his homework, pal. And don't stare,' she ordered, under her breath. The tension was growing in the pit of her stomach and the headache showed no signs of responding to the two aspirins she had taken. She wanted to make a good impression and Ben looked fairly tidy in his white shirt and red blazer. She had chosen a plain but well cut linen suit, a pleasing shade of blue, and with it a cream silky blouse that tied at the neck with a floppy bow. She had put up her hair in an attempt to look mature . . . as Mr Hicks had pointed out, to sixty-year-olds, girls in their early twenties were hardly adults.

'Can you see anyone who looks remotely like our Professor?' she added, looking round the lounge with quickening heartbeat.

'Could this be him, do you think?' Ben pinched her arm and she followed his gaze eagerly. A small, elderly man with fuzzy grey hair was coming towards them, a smile of welcome on his face.

'Oh, yes,' breathed Alex in relief. Surely she could handle this funny old thing! About to put on her most winsome smile, she saw with acute disappointment that he was passing them by.

'Miss Templar?'

The voice came from somewhere above her right shoulder. Alex swung round and froze.

'Miss Alexandra Jane Templar, of Norwich, England?'

The colour surged into her face and as quickly receded. The cool, penetrating grey eyes bored relentlessly into her own, and even as her bewildered thoughts battened on to the hope that it was all a

ghastly mistake, Ben stepped in with the direct sim-
plicity of the child he was.

'Hullo,' he said shyly. 'Are you Professor Devlin?'

'I am,' the Professor replied gravely. 'And you are
Ben. How do you do, Ben?' and he held out his hand
which was large, strong and weather-worn.

Alex found her voice. 'B-but you can't be!' she
protested faintly, face now pale, emphasising the
shadows smudged delicately beneath her eyes.

A dark brow lifted and his eyes, which had been
warm and kind for Ben now hardened. 'Can't I?
Surely you were expecting me?'

Alex's heart sank like a stone. He was angry, very
angry, and nothing was going right, and of course she
hadn't been expecting him!

Ben grinned delightedly. 'We thought you'd be old,
like Father! We thought that was you,' and he indicated
the little old man.

'I see. You were expecting an ancient fuddy-duddy,
were you? I'm sorry to disappoint you.'

Ben shook his head, a lock of fair hair falling across
his brow. 'Oh, no, I'm glad you're you,' he replied
ingenuously. 'Aren't you, Alex?' and he turned a
happy face to his sister.

'Yes. Yes, of course,' stammered Alex, and the Professor allowed himself the knowledge of her existence
once more.

'Your sister is not so sure, Ben.'

The smooth, silky voice stabbed at her senses and
Alex pulled herself together.

'I'm sorry,' she said, 'you must think us very silly.
We were expecting someone more in keeping with the
popular idea of a professor.' She held out a slim,
gloved hand. 'How do you do, Professor Devlin.' The
big brown hand touched hers briefly and she managed

a tremulous smile. 'I think you must be awfully young to be a professor.'

'I'm thirty-four, Miss Templar. Not so young.' The reply was polite. His gaze swept over the pile of luggage waiting on a nearby trolley. 'Is that yours?' and receiving a helpful 'yes' from Ben, he went on: 'Wait here while I deal with it,' and he left them, his long, easy stride taking him quickly towards one of the porters.

Ben gave a chuckle. 'Alex, isn't he great! He's not a bit like I imagined him, is he you?'

'Not even in my wildest dreams,' Alex answered heavily, thinking bitterly that he didn't even dress like a professor. Faded khakis, canvas shoes, a ranger hat tipped to the back of his head, a white crisp shirt open at the neck to reveal a deeply tanned throat. She sighed and put fingertips to forehead. If she wasn't careful she was going to pass out at his feet, and that she was determined not to do.

'The luggage is being put in the car. Let's go, shall we?'

He was back. Her eyes flew open and she stiffened her spine. As they passed from the cool, air-conditioned airport building the heat outside hit them like a blast from a furnace. Ben shot into the back of the waiting car, a black Pontiac, and Nicholas Devlin turned to Alex, blocking her passage.

'You look pale. Are you ill?'

It was a few seconds before her eyes adjusted to the glare of the sun and she squinted up at the tall figure standing before her. The question was a mere formality and she addressed the third button down on the open-neck shirt.

'I'm perfectly all right, thank you.' The words were a hollow repetition of the previous night. She waited for him to step aside and then she joined Ben in the back, wincing as the heat from the upholstery came up to meet her.

Devlin slid his large frame into the passenger seat and waved a hand at the young Thai sitting behind the wheel.

'This is Rachan. You'll be dealing with each other quite a lot. Rachan, this is Miss Alex and Master Ben.'

The Thai beamed a smile of greeting and then deftly edged the Pontiac into the queue of traffic waiting to leave the airport.

Nicholas Devlin half-turned in his seat, his arm stretched across its back, his attention equally divided between the road ahead and his passengers. The sleeves of his jacket were rolled back to the elbow showing an expanse of tanned skin covered with fine dark hairs, a freckle or two, and an old scar running from midway to the wrist bone. His hand lay curved on the leather upholstery. Alex knew the strength of those hands—had bruises to prove it.

'More travelling for you both, I'm afraid, but airports must necessarily be some distance from cities for safety,' he was explaining to Ben. 'It's about twenty-five kilometres to the centre of Bangkok . . . that's fifteen miles in English measurement.'

Fifteen miles! Alex gritted her teeth.

'Are they supposed to drive like that?' Ben asked in awe as he took in the sight of cars zooming both sides of the Pontiac.

Devlin laughed. 'You'll get used to it. Not to worry, Rachan is very competent. The rule is to drive on the left, but from then on it's every man for himself.' He paused. 'You must have found the orderly traffic of Singapore more to your liking. What made you change your mind and go there first?' This was directed to

Alex, but Ben jumped in brightly:

'It rained and rained and was horrid. Alex had to walk through the floods!'

'I think Professor Devlin already knows about the floods, Ben,' Alex said stonily. 'We wanted to visit Father's grave,' she added, giving him a fleeting look before closing her eyes, all effort concentrating on enduring the journey.

Looking back, her first impressions of Bangkok were heat, noise, smiling brown faces, tall office and hotel blocks, dust and bright garish colours.

'Here we are.'

Alex gave a sigh of relief as they approached an iron gateway which opened to allow them entry into a pretty courtyard shaded by trees. The car swept in a semi-circle, coming to a halt outside the entrance to a tall, white apartment building. In the centre of the courtyard was a grassy area dotted with flower beds and tubs bearing miniature trees and shrubs. Rachan shot out of his seat and ran round the back of the Pontiac.

Devlin murmured: 'Always allow him to open the door for you, Miss Templar. If you don't, he'll feel he's lost face.'

Alex gave Rachan a quick smile of thanks as she removed herself from the back seat. Her legs felt like cotton wool and a hand gripped her arm, compelling her to the shade of the trees.

'Hang on for a mite longer, Miss Templar. We wouldn't want the stiff British Upper Lip to collapse in front of the natives, would we?' and waiting briefly to see that she could stand, Nicholas Devlin walked back to the car. Alex clamped her jaw together and glared at the receding khaki back.

'There's a swimming pool, Alex,' pronounced Ben

with satisfaction, having explored the courtyard. The luggage was now stacked by the lift and Ben drew Alex towards the building. 'Just imagine! We'll be living in a flat with a lift and a pool!' His voice showed glee.

'You'll have to get used to saying elevator, not lift, and apartment, not flat, out here, Ben,' Nicholas Devlin remarked, as he pressed the button for the sixth floor.

Bossy, arrogant Americans, thought Alex, fixing the man with a stony stare. Bossy, arrogant, too young professors!

'Don't they speak English here, then?' asked Ben, and Nicholas Devlin smiled.

'Oh, yes, but most Thais have learnt their English from Americans, you see.'

'You sound a bit American yourself,' offered Ben shyly.

'Well, I guess you're right. My mother is American, you see,' and then the lift stopped and they walked out on to a square landing.

The main door to the apartment now opened and a tiny woman scuttled out, smiling and bowing and making a *wai* to each of them in turn. Her eyes, dark and almond-shaped, peeped up with avid interest at the brother and sister as they entered.

'This is Malee,' said Nicholas Devlin, 'and she lives in. Anything you want when I'm not here, you ask her. Malee, this is Miss Alex and Master Ben. We're all thirsty, so can you make us a glass of your excellent *Nam manao*, please?'

'Yes, master.' Malee hurried barefoot across the polished wood floor into the kitchen. Rachan followed them in, carrying the cases, which he took into two rooms and then left as silently as he had come.

Nicholas Devlin turned to Alex, saying: 'There are

things we have to discuss, but they can wait if you
want to lie down for a while.'

'No, thank you. I prefer to talk now,' replied Alex.

He gave her a long look and then nodded thoughtfully.

'Stubborn as well as haughty,' he murmured. 'Ben,
suppose you find your swimming trunks and try out
the pool? You can swim?'

'Yes, sir,' admitted Ben, liking the suggestion.

'Good. Here's your room,' and the Professor opened
one of the doors off, Ben following and peering inside.
'Your sister's room is this one next to it and you'll
share the connecting bathroom.' He indicated the two
doors opposite. 'That's my room and the main bathroom.'

Ben walked slowly into his room, his eyes taking in
the bunk beds with their bright blue covers, the desk,
the bookshelves. 'This is nice,' he said shyly.

'I'm glad you think so. I will admit to having taken
trouble over it. We'll try and serve each other well, eh,
Ben?'

Ben flushed slightly but held his guardian's searching look, replying gruffly: 'Yes, sir.'

'Well, now—hurry and get your things. There's a
towel in the bathroom you can use.' Returning to the
main room, Nicholas Devlin said dryly: 'I seem to be
making a habit of offering towels to the Templar
family.' Alex was still standing just inside the door
where he had left her, strands of hair hanging limply
round her pale face. She looked, he thought, a mixture
of vulnerability and aggression. 'Are you sure you
wouldn't like to join Ben in a swim first?' he asked
mildly. 'It's quite pleasant at this time of the day. You
can swim, I take it?'

'If you'd let me fall in that damn monsoon drain

you'd know, wouldn't you?' she retorted blightingly.

'Rather a drastic way of finding out, though, don't you think?' he drawled.

Alex could have wept. 'This is a ridiculous situation,' she burst out mutinously, 'and . . .'

'No more ridiculous and far less disturbing,' he cut in scathingly, 'than you spending the night in a stranger's hotel bedroom. I suppose you were going to keep quiet about that?'

'I'm not answerable to you,' Alex protested, her voice low, very conscious of Ben in the next room. 'You're not my guardian, and . . .'

'No, I'm not your guardian, thank God, but I am Ben's. Am I supposed to condone an eight-year-old left alone in a strange hotel?' he asked icily, the grey eyes cold and hard.

'That's not fair! And he was being looked after—I'd arranged that. He was perfectly safe.'

'That's comforting to know,' came the heavy reply. 'And you? Were you perfectly safe?' The sarcasm was unmistakable.

'You should know,' she retorted, adding crossly, 'You know I was.'

'Really? More by good luck than management, I feel.'

'Perhaps you're worried about the kiss? Don't worry, I won't hold that against you . . .' and there was a defiant taunt in her voice.

His head came round at that, eyes narrowed, mouth a straight line. 'The man you met in Singapore, Miss Templar, is quite different from the one you see standing before you now—get that into your head! Last night you were a stranger, someone I'd never meet again and whose memory would die very quickly.'

Alex turned away and stared out of the window. He waited a moment and continued in the same controlled voice.

'The minute you signed your full name at the bottom of that letter things changed. No longer were you anonymous—you were Charles Templar's daughter. No stranger—but someone under my care and protection while you're in this country,' and when he saw her back stiffen, he went on: 'Yes, I know I'm not your guardian, you seem very insistent about that, and with no less relief than my own, I might add, but while you are my guest I am your sponsor, so far as the Thai immigration is concerned.' He moved slightly and eyed her profile. 'I am, whether you like the idea or not, responsible for you. James Hicks should never have allowed you to change the plans—but then the poor man is probably easily twisted round your little finger. Well, Alexandra Jane, you won't be able to manipulate me so easily.'

Alex flicked him a disdainful look and renewed her vigilance of the rooftops of Bangkok.

He regarded her, head slightly to one side. 'Now I know why you seemed familiar to me. You have a look of Charles.'

'I'm supposed to take after my mother,' Alex said stonily.

'Perhaps it's as well I've had a few hours to simmer down,' he said repressively, and then caught sight of Ben coming from his room, met him half-way and smiled. 'You look ready for action. And here's Malee with the drinks—thank you, Malee. Yes, you can take one down with you, Ben.' Nicholas Devlin looked him over. 'You'll have to take care in the sun, but there's no worry at this time of the day. Come along, I'll hand you over to Rachan.'

Ben flashed Alex a quick grin as they passed and she heard the Professor talking to Rachan, who had been waiting in the hall. She took one of the drinks, sipping it tentatively at first and then drinking it down appreciatively. *Nam manao* was obviously made from fresh lemons and limes.

Now that she was alone Alex looked round the apartment more closely. It was planned round one huge room with windows at each end, both leading out on to a balcony. There were potted plants and garden furniture on the front balcony and on the rear a washtub, mangle and clothes line. The view from both windows was of blue skies, white stucco buildings and tropical vegetation.

Above her head swirled four fans, the donors of a slight breeze, the general coolness provided by an air-conditioning unit, humming away in a box high up on one wall. The decor was white—cool, fresh, spotless.

It was a pleasant, airy room, well polished and comfortable. Mellow wood combined with cane and rattan and a leather suite was filled with cushions in muted browns and beiges. Books lined floor-to-ceiling shelves and a writing desk stood in one corner looking well used, overflowing with folders, papers and an uncovered typewriter.

As her eyes travelled the room she found that Professor Devlin collected pictures, statues, pottery, tapestries and beautifully carved wood. Some of them looked old and fragile and were probably valuable. Alex was drawn to the statue of a Buddha. He was in bronze, a slim figure, seated crosslegged on the coiled body of a serpent, one hand in his lap, the other raised, palm outwards. On his face was an expression of peace and serenity and Alex thought him quite beautiful. She heard the door close and turned to find the Professor had returned. As he came over to collect his drink he nodded at the statue.

'So you are admiring my Buddha? Not to be confused with the Chinese Buddha who is fat and round—the Thai Buddha is a slim, graceful fellow.' He took a long, thirsty drink and added: 'By the way, you needn't worry about Ben, Rachan will keep an eye on him.'

Alex shrugged a shoulder and replied with supreme unconcern: 'I wouldn't have let Ben go if I'd thought there was any danger. He can swim like a fish.'

There was a long pause and then Nicholas Devlin replaced his glass carefully.

'When you know me better, you'll realise that I never leave anything to chance, but it was good of you to tell me, Alexandra. For you won't always be around to put me right, will you?' The threat was deliberate and unmistakable.

Alex was the first to drop her eyes, a cold fear clutching at her heart. What a fool she was to show her claws to this man, and to let her personal feelings cloud her judgment!

'Don't play games with me, my girl, you'll only get hurt,' Nicholas Devlin was saying softly. 'Now I suggest, if we can, that we start from scratch, here and now. Singapore was bad luck for you, I can see that. Well, we'll try and forget Singapore.' He took her arm and led her to one of the armchairs. 'Sit down before you fall down. Have you taken something for that headache?'

Alex nodded and remarked defensively: 'You said your name was Patrick.'

'So it is. My given name is Patrick Nicholas Devlin, but I'm called Nicholas to avoid confusion with my father, who is also a Patrick.' He turned to lean against the desk, arms folded across his chest. 'It never occurred to me that you would assume I was the same age as your father. Did he never speak of our friendship?'

'We didn't even know you existed, Professor Devlin,' she answered shortly.

'I was twenty-two when Charles came to Cambridge to give a series of lectures,' he mused. 'They drastically changed the direction of my life, influencing me more than any other single event. I was convinced then that he was a brilliant scholar and in the ensuing years I've had no occasion to change my views. For a period we worked together as colleagues and have kept in touch by the occasional letter or meeting.' He paused, his words coming out slowly. 'I feel his loss deeply, both on a personal level as well as a professional one.'

'When did you see him last?' Alex made her voice casual.

Devlin pondered a moment. 'About nine months ago, in Stockholm. I was asked to read a paper there and your father was present.'

'His will was dated six months ago. Did he ask you about Ben when you saw him?'

He considered before replying calmly: 'He made no mention of either of you but I think he must have had knowledge that he was not a well man, looking back. Charles was working on a book at the time and wanted a chapter on the hill tribes in Thailand. I agreed to collaborate with him and he made some remark, a joke almost, saying I was the only person he would trust with his manuscript and if anything happened to him would I see it published.'

'How like my father,' burst in Alex bitterly, colour flooding her face, 'to tag Ben on to the manuscript as an afterthought! Don't you see, we have no claim on you?'

'No, I don't see it like that. Your father chose me to guard his son until he becomes a man. There is a moral claim so far as I am concerned. I don't believe Charles did this lightly. I fully concede that my guardianship will be no easy undertaking, but I accept it as something I have to do—want to do, for Charles's sake.'

Alex turned away in disgust, the words tumbling out. 'Oh, isn't that just like an academic! You scholars are all the same! A moral claim! Never mind about the little boy who has to be uprooted and . . .'

His hands came out and forced her round. 'Alexandra, I fully understand your distress, but though I've no wish to cause you more pain, I believe the time has come when Ben will be served the better for male supervision.' He looked down at her set, white face. 'It's possible that Charles thought the same.'

'I disagree! So long as we were no trouble he left us alone!'

'Whatever the reasons for your father's way of life it seems a pity that Ben should be influenced by his sister's bitterness,' Nicholas Devlin observed evenly.

'That's not fair! I've done my utmost to keep Ben's respect for our father! You don't understand . . . you're saying things now that . . .' Her voice failed and she broke away, hands to face, furious with herself for breaking down.

He waited a moment and then said: 'You're young, attractive and intelligent. Might not your father have considered the possibility of you marrying? There aren't many men who would be willing to take on another man's responsibilities in the form of a young brother.'

'I would never have abandoned Ben—never! My father should have known that,' Alex replied scornfully, her head coming round to show cheeks wet with tears.

'Perhaps he did know. Perhaps he did this for your sake as much for Ben's' He paused. 'Is there no ardent lover left behind in England?'

'I really don't see that . . .'

'Then you're a fool,' he told her bluntly. 'My dear girl, at your age you should be worrying over your own babies. Ben will be leaving the nest without a backward glance in a few years' time. What will you do then?'

'You make me out a stranger to myself,' she accused, raising fingertips to forehead, trying to think above the thumping of her head. 'You're charging me with stifling Ben, smothering him with an unnatural love. It's not like that . . .'

'Maybe not at the moment.'

'I've known all about the pitfalls you're insinuating. I've tried my hardest not to be too protective—no real mother could have been more careful.'

'And now we come to the crux of the matter,' Nicholas said carefully. 'You may have done all you say, but you're not his mother, and never will be. You're his sister.'

'I've never thought of myself as anything else,' Alex ground out as if battling with an idiot.

Antagonistic silence stretched between them. Nicholas broke it.

'I understand your mother died when you were fourteen, a few days after Ben's birth.'

Alex nodded. 'My father was out of the country at the time.'

He chose to ignore the implied criticism. 'You were

too young to look after Ben. Who did?'

She looked at him pityingly. 'A succession of house-keepers.'

'A succession?'

'As soon as they began to imagine themselves as mistress of the house instead of keeper-cum-nurse they were told to go. You will agree that even at the age of sixty my father was still a good-looking man.'

'I see.'

'I wonder if you do, Professor Devlin,' she said rather wearily, and then her eyes were caught by the sight of a photograph propped up on the desk behind him. It was a family group, Nicholas Devlin with a pretty fair-haired girl and a baby of about a year. He followed her look and said quietly:

'My wife and child.'

Alex adjusted to this piece of information and asked abruptly:

'And will your wife be a mother to Ben, Professor? How does she feel on moral issues?'

'I'm a widower. My wife and child died some years ago.'

'Oh! I'm sorry,' she said faintly. 'I didn't know.'

'Why should you? It has no bearing on the case. Your father's wishes are cut and dried, wife or no wife.' For a moment the fans were the only sound in the room.

'I should like to wash and change my clothes,' Alex stated coldly.

He inclined his head. 'Of course.' He moved towards the door, pushing it open so that she could walk past. 'If there's anything you require, please don't hesitate to ask,' he said politely.

'Thank you, I won't need anything,' Alex told him dismissively, and found herself caught by the arm as she passed and winced as the iron grip found one of her bruises from the night before.

'I shall try and make your stay here as pleasant as I can, but I shall need some co-operation from you . . . and not only for Ben's sake. If I consider that your presence here is a disruptive influence I shall have no hesitation in despatching you back to England.' He paused. 'Do you understand?' Alex gave the briefest of nods. He released her and turned on his heel, closing the door behind him with exact precision.

Alex stood for a moment without moving, a great weariness sweeping over her. Her eyes wandered round the room, over the twin beds with their pretty pink spreads, the gay floral curtains, the bowl of flowers on the dressing-table. At any other time the room would have been welcoming and delightful. She saw that the flowers were orchids.

Nicholas Devlin was standing staring out of the window. By the look on his face his thoughts were not pleasant ones. Whatever their nature, however, they were brought to an abrupt end by the sound of a stran-gled cry from within the room he had recently vacated. In a few quick strides he reached the door and flung it open, the impetus of his movement taking him a couple of yards inside. He swept a hard, searching look round the room, brow lowered, muscles tensed for action, then his head came round to Alex, clutch-ing the soft material of her discarded blouse to her slip-clad figure. He relaxed slightly, an eyebrow wing-ing up in question.

'There's a c-creature in my room,' she gasped, taken aback by the suddenness of his entry. 'It scuttled across the ceiling and . . . down the wall.' She pointed quickly. 'There! See?' She swung back and saw him visibly relax and added lamely: 'It's gone behind the bed.'

Her host nodded and put his hands thoughtfully in his pockets.

'Hmm ... yes, well, that's a gecko. He's quite a harmless little chap.'

A faint flush tinged her cheeks. 'A gecko?' she echoed feebly, rapidly coming to the conclusion that she was a fool and wishing the ground would open up and swallow her.

'Yes. A small, lizard-like creature, invaluable round the house as an insect eater. You'll find them everywhere.'

'Really?' came the flat reply.

'You'll not even notice them when you've been here a few days,' Nicholas assured her blandly.

If there had been any hint of amusement in those damn grey eyes she would have grabbed the nearest antique, priceless or not, and thrown it at him. There wasn't. He was an intuitive man. With her hair tumbling round her shoulders and in a vulnerable state of undress she was left with only her dignity to fall back on. Lifting her chin, she said:

'I'm sure you're right,' and the bossy, arrogant professor replied mildly:

'I usually am.' He walked to the door and turned. 'I'll send Malee in with something for those bruises,' and with a short nod, he left the room.

Alex looked at the closed door for some seconds and suddenly finding that she was still clutching the silk blouse, threw it with all her force, watching its soft contact against the wood and subsequent fall to the floor.

She gave a short, silent laugh. How very symbolic! Silk against wood. If she were in an imaginative frame of mind it would be easy to liken the impact of herself against dear Professor Devlin in such terms.

Well, maybe ... but silk was tougher than it looked!

CHAPTER THREE

ALEX woke to find the sun on her face. The clock on the bedside table said eight o'clock, and as amazement swept through her the bottle of wych-hazel standing next to it reminded her vividly that what was supposed to have been a short rest had taken her through the night! She was still in her slip. Someone had come in and covered her over with a lightweight quilt.

She lay for a few moments assessing the situation, knowing it wasn't good. Only a naïve optimist would equate the real Professor Nicholas Devlin with that shadowy figure of a man she had hoped to persuade to her plan of taking Ben back to England. It was going to be very, very difficult to make this man change his mind about anything. She gave a sigh. What a mess everything was! Nothing had gone right so far.

The wych-hazel caught her eye again and she sat up and studied the bruises on her upper arms. They were turning a nice colour. Swinging herself out of the bed, Alex rummaged in the case until she found a dress with short sleeves. It would be politic to cover up those tell-tale signs if Singapore needed to be forgotten.

Ben was on the balcony eating breakfast when she emerged, bathed and dressed in a simple button-through cotton dress of brown candy-stripe. Malee was pouring orange juice and seeing Alex gave a beaming smile, saying shyly:

'Missy have breakfast now?'

'Yes, please, Malee—just fruit and coffee will do

nicely, thank you,' replied Alex with an answering smile, sitting down at the table and looking out at the view. She wondered if the novelty of being able to sit outside at eight o'clock in the morning, in October, would ever wear off when it was no longer a novelty. And following this up with the thought that she wouldn't be here long enough to find out she brought her attention back to her brother, now tucking into a large bowl of fresh pineapple. 'How long have you been up?' she asked him, her eyes flitting beyond the balcony doors, wishing she could get this next meeting with the Professor over and done with.

'Ages. This is smashing, Alex, do try some.'

'I shall. I can see it's juicy. Wipe your chin. Where's Professor Devlin?'

'He's gone . . . he went about half an hour ago. They start work early here, while it's cool, and finish earlier. Nick says . . .'

'Nick?' questioned Alex sharply. 'Is that what you call him?'

'Uhuh . . . he told me to, said it was more friendly. We had a great chat through dinner last night.' Ben grinned wickedly. 'Nick said you looked as though you were out for a hundred years! Like the Sleeping Beauty! So we left you.'

So it had been the Professor who had covered her over with the quilt.

'Nick says we're to spend a lazy day by the pool and not to get sunburnt. He'll be home about four.'

'Then we'll do as Nick says,' answered Alex mildly.

It had been no part of her plans to be asleep when he came. By four o'clock the shadows of the palm trees had lengthened and half-covered the pool, making it pleasantly cool to swim in. Alex had swum, on and off, and had apportioned herself and Ben only a minimum amount of time in direct sunshine, knowing how easily they became burnt. Ben was now playing with another boy from the apartment at Scrabble on one of the round tables shielded by a coloured umbrella. Alex had pulled her lounger into the shade, spreading her hair out like a fan to dry, and had merely closed her eyes for a minute, soaking up the heat and thinking how marvellous it would be if this visit was merely a holiday one.

A few spots of water on her bare flesh woke her and she found Nicholas towelling himself off as he watched Ben and his new friend dive for his benefit into the far end of the pool. Then his glance slanted down at her and the encouraging expression changed to a mocking one, the grey eyes, enjoying her discomfort, were amused.

'Asleep again?' He looked the picture of health and vitality as he stood, towel in hand, hair tousled, droplets of water coursing down his body. He was tanned and very hairy and as he bent to rub his legs the muscles in his arms became taut. Alex averted her gaze to the pool, ostensibly laughing at Ben attempting the butterfly stroke but all the while terribly aware of the man by her side.

'How do you feel today? Has Malee been looking after you?' Nicholas pulled a chair over and sat down, raking a hand through his hair before turning his regard on her, eyes hidden by half-closed lids.

'Malee has been sweet and has looked after us beautifully, thank you.' Alex sat up and swung her legs round, reaching for her wrap. 'And I'm feeling fine.'

'Good.' His eyes swept over her. 'I'm glad you've been sensible and stayed out of the sun. Don't run away, Alex. I want to talk to you.'

Her chin came up and she gave him one of her

haughtiest looks. 'I have no intention of running away,' and then Ben dragged himself from the pool and plodded over, panting for breath and scattering them with water. Alex was glad of the diversion. Damn the man! He was too astute for words. She had been about to escape into the apartment and was furious with herself for allowing this . . . ape of a man to make her feel so gauche! Men had seen her in a bikini before, for goodness' sake! Why should Nick Devlin have this humiliating effect on her? and as quickly as she asked the question she came back grimly with the answer—power. She and Ben were both in his hands and his assurance and authority were undermining her own. She set her mouth obstinately. Well, every man had his Achilles' heel . . . she would just have to find out where the Professor was most vulnerable.

'I think now is as good a time as any for me to tell you a few dos and don'ts to make life easier and healthier for you both during your stay here.' He leaned back in the chair, face serious. 'Firstly, you must always remember that Thailand is an Eastern country, with customs and a way of living that will be strange and sometimes difficult for you to accept. There are certain things necessary for you to know, as guests on her soil, both for your safety and so that you don't offend. Do you understand?' He paused and waited and Ben nodded quickly, and his eyes flicked briefly to Alex, who murmured: 'Of course.' The reply, not the assurance, satisfied him, but he continued evenly: 'We'll start with the water. You must always use bottled water, even for cleaning your teeth. You'll find a flask by your bed which Malee will keep permanently filled. The tap water is safe to wash in, but not to drink. *Farangs* who ignore this advice can expect to suffer from Bangkok tummy.'

'*Farang?*' asked Alex, interested despite herself.

'The Thai word for a Westerner.'

'What's a Bangkok tummy?' Ben enquired, and Nicholas said dryly:

'A bad pain,' and Ben grinned, suddenly understanding. Alex caught the amused glance the Professor shot him and felt a stab of jealousy, which instantly shocked her.

'Food at the apartment,' Devlin was saying, 'can be eaten without reserve, Malee has been well trained in Western standards, but I'd rather you didn't buy from the street vendors without bringing it home to wash first. The fruit, for instance, will look clean, but will have been washed in the klong or the river. Thai peasants wash themselves, their clothing, possessions and their food, all in the klong.'

'I'm glad you told us,' Alex observed equably. If he had hoped to disconcert her he was mistaken.

'It doesn't affect the Thais, of course, they become immune. In no circumstances are you to touch any stray dogs. There's no quarantine laws or restrictions of any kind and consequently there's always a serious threat of rabies. And then there are pickpockets—as *farangs* you're an obvious source of income.'

Alex broke in dryly: 'They'll be disappointed if they try me—I haven't anything to put in my pockets. Will you tell me what we do about money?'

Devlin gave an exclamation of annoyance. 'Yes, of course—forgive me, I should have brought that question up before now.' He stood up and began to collect the towels. 'Let's go back up and I'll give you both a lesson on the currency.' They followed him and made their way back to the apartment where he fetched his wallet and laid a selection of paper notes on the table, all varying colours.

'Thai currency is called *baht*, pronounced bart, and the rate of exchange at the moment is approximately two hundred *baht* to your pound sterling. It comes in notes and silver coins.'

'It looks like Monopoly money,' said Ben.

Devlin smiled, and then turned to Alex. 'I'll let you have some cash now. There's been a sum transferred from your father's estate to the bank here from which you can draw, on an allowance basis. Your Mr Hicks will explain the money side of things to you more fully when you return to England.' At these words there was silence and then Ben said:

'Are you going to send Alex away?' His voice quivered and the blood drained from his face. Alex gripped the edge of the table, waiting for the reply, hating her father for putting them in this position and Nick Devlin for being her father's instrument.

Nicholas regarded Ben calmly and his voice was unhurried: 'No, I'm not sending her away, Ben, you've only just arrived. But things never stay the same, you know, and . . .'

'Alex has always looked after me!' Ben flung himself round and threw himself on to his sister. 'Alex, you promised me we'd be together!'

'And you are,' Nicholas pointed out reasonably before she could speak, 'so why are you getting upset? Alex won't leave without your agreement, I promise you.'

There was a long pause and then Ben relaxed. 'That's all right, then,' and rather sheepishly he trailed his towel into his room. When the door closed behind him Devlin said grimly:

'Just what have you been promising that boy, Alex Templar?'

'Nothing! Since we knew the terms of my father's

will, I've promised nothing,' she retorted, keeping her voice low, her body rigid with anger. 'Do you think me stupid?'

'No, merely emotionally involved.'

'That's better than being without any emotion at all!' she answered bitterly. 'I may have made promises earlier, yes, I'm sure I did, when we first heard of my father's death. But that was because I thought we'd be staying together.' She swung round and said with controlled calmness, 'You won't find it easy to get rid of me, Professor Devlin. I'll find some way of staying here in Thailand, never fear.'

'You will stay as my guest for just so long as I say,' he replied. 'I would remind you once again that I'm your sponsor and you will do as you're told.' He was quite unruffled by her outburst and she thrust her hands in the pockets of her robe, seething inwardly.

'And I would remind you, Professor Devlin, that I have eight years' experience of bringing up a child.' Her eyes flicked to the photograph on his desk and as she saw the happy, laughing face of the baby boy her resolve nearly faltered. And then she remembered Ben's white face and continued: 'What similar experience have you to offer, Professor?' She allowed herself one casual glance at his face and pivoted on her heel, walking to her room, outwardly cool, inwardly shaken. Once inside she leant back against the door and let out a long-held breath. Had the Professor's profile been carved in granite it couldn't have been more stone-like. Oh, yes, he had his Achilles' heel, all right. All she needed was the strength to do battle.

Bangkok was, thought Alex, a city of changing faces. There was the clear, fresh face of early morning, warm and pleasant like an English summer's day. This was followed by the bright, harsh face of midday, when it was necessary to seek out the shade of a tree or the cool of the apartment. Dusk was a more muted heat, the daylight falling quickly with little warning, to be followed by night—warm, black and mysteriously exciting.

It was the evening of their second day and they were travelling through the city in the Pontiac on their way to a charity dinner-dance. Nicholas was driving, Ben by his side, with Alex sitting in the back. She was nervous and trying not to show it. This was to be their first introduction into Thai society and she knew intuitively that it would be an ordeal. With that knowledge in mind she had dressed Ben and herself with care, the boy wearing a white casual shirt and grey lightweight trousers. He still looked young for his age, but his ability to fall prey to any germ going round was lessening with the years. For herself she had chosen a fine pleated dress of pale turquoise chiffon, mainly for the long, loose sleeves, for the bruises on her arms were still visible. Strappy sandals with high heels gave her a few extra inches and she had left her hair to hang free.

Her eyes moved to her host. There was polite restraint between them, an unspoken agreement of keeping up appearances in front of Ben, but nothing was altered beneath the surface. Despite their enmity she found a perverse satisfaction that the turquoise chiffon was able to hold its own beside the white dinner jacket, midnight blue silk shirt and dark trousers of knife-edge crease.

'There's the Grand Palace,' said Ben, picking out the distinctive skyline of tiered roofs rising high behind the tall white wall surrounding the compound. As they drove by Alex remembered their visit to the

Royal Palace and Emerald Buddha Temple that morning. Ben was chattering away to his guardian about what he had seen, asking questions and receiving patient replies. The architecture and sense of history had passed over his head, but there was much to excite a little boy's imagination—gigantic, colourful statues of dragons, monkey-faced men, elephants and lions, creatures half human, half bird, and warriors with white faces and pointed helmets.

Alex had walked round the Palace and temples hardly able to believe her eyes. It seemed like a world of make-believe, a fairy story. Colour predominated over everything. Roofs were of startling blues, yellows, greens and oranges, doors were mother-of-pearl mosaic, porcelain flowers decorated walls and pillars and everywhere there was the sparkle of gold—gold Buddhas, gold thrones, gold pagodas and statues. It was too much to take in on one visit.

'The snake is called *Naga*,' Devlin was telling Ben, 'and you'll find him on all temples and ceremonial buildings, along with the giants, the *yaks*. Both are mythical creatures, of course, and interwoven into all Thai legends.' He glanced into the mirror and found Alex listening. 'I'll look out a phrase book and you can learn some basic Thai words. In Bangkok you'll find that most shopkeepers and cab drivers can speak English reasonably well, especially the hotels who cater for tourists. Street vendors know enough to trade. Up country in the rural areas it will be only spoken by a few.'

'What are these children doing?' Ben asked curiously, as the car slowed for traffic lights. Alex followed his look and saw a group of children, some only Ben's age, darting along the line of cars, offering their wares.

'They make their living selling newspapers, fruit, flowers. Tonight being Loy Krathong, they're selling *krathongs*.'

'I helped Malee make my *krathong*, Alex,' Ben told his sister, turning in his seat to look at the flower and leaf arrangement lying on the vacant place in the back. 'Isn't it pretty? Malee did the bottom bit because it was difficult,' he admitted, 'you have to weave the moss and leaves together and mine kept falling apart. But I stuck the flowers in, and the candle. It's a bit wobbly, do you think it will fall over, Alex?'

Alex tested it with a tentative finger and said: 'No, I think it will be all right.' The car began to move again. 'What does Loy Krathong mean?'

'The Water Candle Festival. *Loy*, to float, *krathong*, bowl of leaves. The candles and incense are lit and the *krathongs* are floated on the water.' Nicholas's eyes flicked to the mirror again and caught the look on her face as they passed the street children. 'They're better off than most, you know. It's no use eating your heart out and trying to compare life out here with life in England. Thailand raises enough food for its people. Those children won't starve, although by your standards they work hard and long hours. It's difficult to accept, I agree, in a city where exotic temples and palaces rub shoulders with corrugated shanties, but that's part of Bangkok's character.'

'They certainly appear to be a race of people who laugh and smile a lot,' agreed Alex, and Nicholas gave a laugh, and shook his head ruefully.

'They have a capacity for enjoyment that's remarkable, you can't help liking the Thais, but that's not to say I can't be driven to exasperation by their easygoing temperament. One of the first phrases a *farang* must learn, Ben, is *mai pen rai*.'

'*Mai pen rai*,' repeated Ben carefully. 'What does it mean, Nick?'

' "That's fate" or "never mind" and is part of the Thai philosophy of life.' Nicholas peered out of the window, easing his foot off the throttle. 'Here we are, Amphorn Gardens, and by the look of things there's quite a crowd here already.' He swung the Pontiac into the car park and they made their way towards the lights.

Alex hadn't known what to expect, but it certainly wasn't this ornamental lake and large building ablaze with lights. People were strolling among the gardens, enjoying the warm night air, and as they came nearer she could see that the majority of guests were Thai, and it seemed to be a family gathering with many children in sight. The Professor was well known, many guests greeting him as they passed by. A paved terrace illuminated by coloured lights led to a flight of steps, beyond which were glass doors opened wide and inside music and voices.

'We're joining friends of mine at their table,' Nicholas murmured to Alex as he showed the large, gold-embossed tickets at the door. A light flashed in their faces and Alex realised they had been photographed, and all she was then aware of was noise and people. She followed Nicholas, grateful for his height and breadth as he shouldered a path through the crowd, and stopped when he did at a round table set in a more secluded corner of the huge hall. There was one person sitting at the table, although there were signs that others had been there earlier—a woman in her early forties. Tanned and slightly plump, she was attractively dressed in a multi-coloured kaftan and her brown, wavy hair was cut short. She saw Nicholas first and her face broke out into a quick smile and she rose instantly to her feet, hands outstretched.

'Nick, my dear, how lovely to see you . . . you've
been neglecting us lately.' She had a low, drawling,
rather attractive American accent, and after giving him
a kiss on the cheek, which he returned, she held back
and eyed him critically. 'You're looking rather tired,
Nick. Too many late nights in Singapore? Is Suzanne
here with you . . .?' and her gaze slipped past him,
lighting on Alex and Ben waiting silently behind him.
Eyes widening for a moment in surprise, she said:
'Well, well, who have we here? Come along, Nick,
introduce me, please!'

Devlin smiled sardonically. 'You've hardly given me
a chance, Mel.' He turned and brought Alex and Ben
forward, one on each arm. 'Mel, I want you to meet
Alexandra and Ben Templar, brother and sister from
England. Alex, Ben, this is Melanie Carr, one half of a
couple of good friends of mine. Where's Warren,
Mel?' he asked, looking round the hall in a futile
attempt to catch sight of his friend.

'Getting drinks,' replied Melanie promptly, as she
shook their hands. She looked Alex frankly up and
down. 'I made a few guesses as to who Nick would be
bringing along this evening, but I never dreamed he'd
bring such a surprise.' Seeing Alex's uncertainty, she
chuckled, adding: 'Forgive me, but we're such a re-
stricted community here in Bangkok that new faces are
the breath of life! You're a sly one, Nick.'

'They only arrived two days ago, Mel,' Nicholas
replied mildly.

'I'll forgive you, then. And what do you think of
Bangkok, Alex?'

'From the little I've seen, it's bewildering, fascinating and beautiful,' answered Alex, and Melanie turned
to Nicholas in delight.

'Nick, just listen to that delicious voice!' and back again to Alex, pulling a wry face: 'There I go again! Don't mind me, my dear, but we get so few Britishers here, mostly Americans, with a smattering of Europeans and Aussies, and I do love listening to a British accent!' She paused. 'And what brings you and your brother to Bangkok?' and seeing Alex look at Nicholas for him to answer, she added dryly: 'Or shouldn't I have asked?'

Before either Nicholas or Alex could reply, Ben said:

'Nick's my guardian.'

Melanie shot Nicholas a startled look and then said: 'Really?'

Ben nodded. 'My father died so there's just me and Alex . . . and now there's Nick.'

'I see.' Melanie arched her brows at this and bent down to Ben and took his hands in hers. 'And how old are you, Ben?'

'Eight.'

'Well now, I have two sons around here somewhere,' and she stood up and peered about, catching the eye of a carrot-haired boy in sweat-shirt, jeans and sneakers, who at a commanding wave came over to join them. 'This is Bud, he's nine, and back there is Johnnie, who's eleven. Bud, this is Ben. Take him over to the film show and look after him, please. You can put your *krathong* under the table with ours, Ben, it'll be quite safe.' She watched the two boys disappear through the crowd and turned to Alex. 'He'll be okay with Bud.'

'Thank you, you're very kind,' murmured Alex, and Melanie gave a strangled yelp of laughter, drawling:

'Hell, no, just wildly curious, but I can restrain myself if necessary. Shall we sit down?' and suiting the

question to the deed she settled herself back in her
chair and Nicholas drew one forward for Alex to
follow suit. 'You certainly are a man of surprises,
Nick. What have you been up to? *You* that boy's guardian? Are you Alex's too?' and before Nicholas could
answer, Alex broke in firmly:

'No, he's not.'

Nicholas said smoothly: 'She may look absurdly
young, Mel, but Alex has reached the ripe old age of
twenty-two, and has no need of a guardian.'

Melanie looked askance at the English girl and
grinned. 'She might have no need, but there are any
number of females here who'd just adore you to be
theirs, Nick! And that reminds me—where's the
beautiful Suzanne?'

'Now why should I know, Mel? Still in Singapore,
probably.'

'Hmm, you're a secretive so-and-so, aren't you? Not
that I blame you, surrounded as we are by so many
vultures,' and seeing Alex's perplexity, Mel smiled
wickedly. 'Gossips, my dear. In such a small white
community it's worse than living in your home town—
nothing's sacred!' She paused, looking from Alex to
Nicholas and back again, breaking out into a chuckle.
'Oh, my, are some folk in for a shock!'

'Behave, Mel,' chided Nicholas affably. 'I'll go and
join Warren at the bar. What would you like, Alex?'

'Martini, please,' she replied, knowing her colour
was high and that Melanie's eyes were still upon her,
'and a fruit drink of some sort for Ben, if they have it.'

'Right, I'll be back,' and Nicholas broke through
the crowd, an easily identifiable figure because of his
size. Both women watched him for a few moments
without speaking, seeing him stop every now and then
to make a *wai* and speak a few words to various Thai

guests who knew him. Melanie was the first to break
the silence.

'Look, my dear, perhaps you'd better tell me how
Nick comes to be your brother's guardian. I'm
genuinely fond of Nick and I'm not exaggerating the
rumours that'll spread quicker than a forest fire in this
place. It's as well if I know the facts so I can squash
the more fancy ones.'

'There's not much to tell,' Alex said awkwardly.
'My mother died when Ben was born and on my
father's death he made Professor Devlin Ben's guardian.' She hesitated, biting her bottom lip. 'Why do
you say there'll be talk?'

'Have one?' Melanie offered a cigarette which Alex
refused with a quick shake of the head. 'You don't?
Wish I didn't, but I'm trying to cut down.' Melanie
drew on the cigarette thoughtfully. 'Nick Devlin is a
difficult man to get to know thoroughly. Oh, a lot of
people think they know him, but he only gives away
what he wants. He annoys the majority of expatriates
here because generally he keeps himself to himself,
and that's not allowed! He's highly thought of by Thai
society—has the entrée to Government circles and has
even been introduced to the King and Queen, so you
see he has some standing in the country. He doesn't
make a song and dance about it, though, and some folk
would like to latch on and bask in reflected glory. And
then he's a highly eligible male, unattached, seemingly
with every intention of staying that way.' She smiled,
her thoughts causing her some amusement as she
added: 'He's no hermit—and although Nick may be an
authority on ruins he sure knows how to pick his lady-
friends, and they're by no means in the same category!
And so when he turns up with you and Ben tongues
are bound to start wagging.'

Under the American woman's speculative gaze Alex found herself blushing.

'That's . . . ridiculous,' she protested with an embarrassed laugh. 'I mean . . . it's just ridiculous!'

'Okay! If you'd turned out to have buck teeth, a squint and a hook nose they mightn't have such a field day.' Melanie clicked her teeth, giving her head a doubtful shake, although her eyes were laughing. 'But you turning out to be the perfect English rose! Well!' She looked at Alex thoughtfully for a moment. 'Say, Alex, that brother of yours looks a little frail. Has he been ill?'

'He was a premature baby, born with two holes in his heart. He still has regular hospital checks, but he's improving all the time,' Alex told her, aware of the sympathy coming from the American.

'Oh, that's tough luck. My own two are sturdy kids, but I can imagine what you've been through.' Melanie patted Alex's hand comfortingly. 'My dear, how relieved you must be to share the responsibility for Ben with a man like Nick. A positive Rock of Gibraltar, and good with boys, too . . . my two adore him, and I'm sure Ben will.'

Alex fought down the impulse to confide in Melanie. It was obvious that she would think her mad to try and break the guardianship. Alex murmured something about being happy to miss an English winter and then Melanie observed:

'Here are our menfolk. Warren,' she called, as her husband drew near, 'if it takes that long to be served, I hope you've brought doubles!'

Warren Carr turned out to be in his late forties. Of medium height, he had bright ginger-red hair and a permanently skinning nose. During the evening Alex found him to be kindly, intelligent and the possessor of a quiet, gentle humour. He worked at the American Embassy.

The Carrs made no demands of her and Alex was able to relax slightly. She was obliged to call the Professor 'Nick', it would have looked too pointed if she had not, and after a while even that became easier. She had to admit that he had gone up in her estimation by the fact of his reticence of their arrival. It would have been distasteful to her had their affairs been common knowledge and bandied about over coffee cups, as Melanie had prophesied.

As they queued up at the tables laden with food Melanie gave her an insight into the life-style of a Western family living and working in a foreign country.

'There are two ways of going about it,' she told Alex. 'Either you throw yourself wholeheartedly into things, learning the country's history, seeking out the culture and getting to know the people, or you live in a tight little community with folk of your own nationality, merely ticking off the days on the calendar until you go back home to what you consider to be civilisation.'

'I gather you belong to the first group,' teased Alex, and Melanie responded emphatically:

'You're right. Now come and sample some of the national delicacies,' she ordered, indicating the array of dishes. She patted her ample hips. 'I ought to give up eating too!'

'Give me a clue,' begged Alex. 'It all looks very mysterious to me, apart from the rice.'

'This is *khao pad*,' a voice said unexpectedly by her side, and Nicholas handed her a plate, 'and it consists of finely diced pork, crab meat and shrimps in fried rice, usually flavoured with garlic and peppers and

served with a fish sauce. Those little red things are
chilli, so be careful, if you're not used to them they
can blow off the top of your head.'

The food was delicious and in abundance. During
the course of the evening Alex was introduced to many
people—no explanations, merely introductions. Nicholas was a charming, polite companion and Alex felt as
though she was sitting in a shop window on full view
of passers-by who did not look in openly, but gave a
quick sideways look as they went past. If Nicholas
noticed he didn't acknowledge the fact.

After the meal came the Thai traditional dancing.
Alex decided that the dancers, with their graceful
hand movements and colourful costumes, pleased her
more than the accompanying music, which she
thought she might have more trouble becoming at-
tuned to.

'We're going to float the *krathongs* now,' Ben said
excitedly, when the music was finished. 'Can I light
the candle and incense stick by myself, Nick?'

Nicholas produced a lighter and when both were lit
Ben carried it carefully and they joined the general
exodus to the gardens.

'We ought to be floating them on the river or a
klong,' observed Warren, helping the boys to reach
down with their *krathongs*. 'It's quite a sight seeing
them float away into the darkness with just the flames
flickering in the dark. Here they'll not move far,
there's no wind.'

Ben squeezed up to his sister, tugging her arm to
attract her attention from Nicholas, who was talking to
a very pretty girl a few yards away.

'They're going to have fireworks, Alex.'

'Oh, are they?' she replied with foreboding, and
edged from the main crowd. She had had a fear of

fireworks ever since childhood and always took evasive action. She was lulled into a false sense of security for a while with some pretty, silent ones, and then the rockets were lit, followed by a jumping-jack, which proved to have spectacular powers of distance. It scattered the crowd in all directions, coming home to roost at Alex's feet. She yelped and leaped backwards, landing on someone behind her.

When the laughing crowd closed up once more she turned to apologise and found herself addressing a Thai, who cut off her apology in fluent English.

'Please, there is no need. I merely saved you from falling, and no, your foot did not land on mine.' He smiled. 'So you are not happy with our firecrackers?'

Alex shook her head ruefully. 'No. It's silly, isn't it?'

'Not at all. Perhaps you would be happier further away, for they haven't finished yet,' and her companion led her to a quiet spot on the steps which gave a good view of the proceedings.

'Thank you, this feels safer,' agreed Alex, surreptitiously studying the man standing by her side, his gaze directed towards the lake. She thought him strikingly handsome, with a pale olive skin, dark almond-shaped eyes, jet black hair and the distinctive high, wide cheekbones of the Oriental. His demeanour was grave and attentive, but when he smiled his air of maturity diminished and if anything, his charm increased.

'Are you entertained by our Loy Krathong?' he asked politely, and Alex smiled.

'It's beautiful. Will you tell me why you float the *krathongs*?'

He inclined his head. 'You must understand that my people have a close relationship with water. It governs two important issues—the means of travel on klong or river, and the production of rice, our main food crop. Loy Krathong is an ancient ceremony and is our annual offering to the water spirits, an expression of gratitude to the Water Goddess for producing the rain so necessary to us. We Thais are a nation that loves any excuse for a festival or holiday.'

'I think it's a lovely idea,' Alex said shyly.

'I trust you will enjoy your stay in my country. You will find it very different from your own.'

'You've been to England?'

He smiled again. 'Many times. I have a high regard for your country. I finished my education at one of your universities.' His attention passed beyond her and his face showed pleasure, and following his look Alex saw Nicholas looming up out of the darkness.

'There you are, Alex.' He walked the steps slowly. 'I wondered where you were,' and turning to her companion, he held out his hand. 'Good evening, Kasem. How are you? I hoped to see you here tonight.'

The Thai clasped the hand with warmth. 'But naturally . . . and where else should I be? I do not shout my presence, Nick, when I am with a beautiful girl. I do not wish to attract attention and thus have her claimed by another.' He smiled. 'But since this has now happened, perhaps, my good friend, you will do me the honour of officially introducing us?'

'I suppose I shall have to,' said Nicholas. 'Alex, allow me to present Kasem Khomang. Kasem, Miss Alexandra Templar, from England.'

'How do you do,' murmured Alex, aware of the contrast between the two men, the American, tall and large, the Thai, smaller and slim.

'My pleasure, Miss Templar.' Kasem gave a slight bow. 'If I can be of any assistance during your stay in

our city, please do not hesitate to let me know. I shall
be most happy to be of service to you.'

'Thank you.'

Kasem addressed Nicholas. 'Varuni made sure that
I tell you she is sad not to be here tonight. She is at
our home in Chiangmai and will be returning to Bangkok within a few days. And now I must leave you.
Sawadee, my friend. Goodnight, Miss Templar.'

Nicholas said: '*Sawadee*, Kasem,' and Alex, returning the *wai* rather selfconsciously with one of her own,
murmured: 'Goodnight.'

On the way home Ben fell asleep and after a desultory conversation Alex asked curiously:

'Who is Varuni? Your friend, Mr ...' and she
frowned, Nicholas coming in helpfully with:

'Khomang, but you must call him Kasem, he will
prefer it. It's rather interesting—surnames have only
been in use here since the beginning of this century.
And Varuni is Kasem's sister. They belong to an old
and highly respected Thai family of jewellers and sil-
versmiths.' Nicholas slowed down at the traffic lights.
'Kasem was probably one of the wealthiest men there
tonight.' He paused and added softly: 'Your children
are still working.'

Alex followed the direction of his gaze. Nicholas
delved into his pocket and wound down the window
just as a boy came along the line. A note was passed.

'Here. To salve your conscience,' and Nicholas
reached across and dropped a necklace of flowers over
her head before returning his attention to the road
ahead.

'They're beautiful,' breathed Alex, burying her face
into the blossoms. 'What are they?'

'Jasmine.' Nicholas gave her a brief glance. 'As for
Varuni, you'll be meeting her yourself soon. She too

speaks good English, having trained at art college in England. You'll like Varuni, she's gentle and kind and very beautiful. She's promised to take you sightseeing.' He swung into the apartment courtyard and pulled to a halt.

Ben woke only sufficiently for Alex to get him to bed. She stood for a moment by his bunk, listening to his quiet breathing, her face contemplative. Varuni. What a lovely name that was. Nicholas's voice had softened whenever he spoke her name, and was there any significance in the fact that he had told Varuni about herself and Ben, yet hadn't told the Carrs, or her brother Kasem? She moved slowly across the room and opened the door. Nicholas was sitting at his desk sorting through a pile of correspondence. In the glow of the single lamp his face seemed drawn and deeply lined. He had taken off his jacket and tie and had rolled back the sleeves of his shirt. Absently he ran a hand through his hair, massaging the back of his neck as though to ease a nagging, persistent ache.

Alex closed Ben's door quietly behind her and remained still, struck by an illuminating insight, unexpected as it was unwanted, into what their presence here was costing him. Responsibility, lack of privacy, a narrowing of activity and the curiosity of others.

Nicholas sensed her presence and looked up, still engrossed, before gathering together his thoughts to say:

'Malee has left fruit and coffee in the kitchen, or would you prefer a nightcap?'

Alex took a few steps forward, uncertain whether he wanted her to stay or go . . . not knowing whether she wanted to stay or go. She shook her head. 'No, thank you, I couldn't manage another thing to eat or drink. Thank you for taking us to Loy Krathong. It's been a lovely evening.'

'I'm glad you enjoyed yourself. I felt you would have an affinity with the Water Goddess, Naiad,' and he gave a lopsided smile and Alex found herself smiling back.

'I liked your friends the Carrs.'

Nicholas crossed to the drinks table, pouring out a measure of whisky, saying as the soda fountain hissed: 'Ben seemed to get on well with the boys, which is pleasing. Bud and Johnnie will be at the same school as Ben and it'll be easier for him if they know each other beforehand.'

The shock of his words couldn't have been more if he had hit her. Fool! Stupid, idiotic fool! She watched in stony silence as he walked back to the desk and began to open more letters, tossing the envelopes into a waste basket and piling the contents neatly in front of him as he talked.

'I've arranged with Mel for her to pick you up tomorrow, about nine-thirty, and she'll take you to Jim Thompson's house. I think you'll find it interesting. Thompson was an American who settled here after the war and was instrumental in bringing Thai silk from a dying-out cottage industry back to a national one. He disappeared rather mysteriously, even now no one appears to know what happened to him, and after ten years his family handed his house over to the Thai people as a museum. He was a prolific collector of antiques.' Suddenly aware of her silence and unnatural stillness, Nicholas looked up, a frown creasing his forehead, grey eyes alert. 'I don't think you've heard one word I've been saying. What's the matter?'

It didn't seem possible that only a few moments ago she had been swept with a feeling of sympathy for this man, and she felt a surge of self-disgust and derision sweep through her. She must have been out of her mind—seeing only what she wanted to see, some weakness, some softness . . . a yielding.

He stood before her, invincible and rock-like, no vulnerability apparent now. The circle of light cast his face in shadow as he moved towards her.

'What have I said to bring that look on your face again?' Narrowing his eyes, Nicholas nodded thoughtfully. 'Ah, yes . . . I have it. Ben and school. It's a very good school, I can assure you, an international one.' One of his hands came up and he lifted her face to his. 'You have very expressive eyes, Alexandra Jane, and they're telling me exactly what you're thinking.' He shook his head slightly. 'I'm sorry, but it seems that I must spell out to you once more that Ben stays here with me. Nothing I've seen so far has made me change my mind about your father's wishes.' With the tip of a finger he drew lightly across the corners of her mouth, which was set obstinately together. 'You have lips made for smiling. They should turn up, not down.' There was a pause. 'Your father trusted me, Alex, why can't you?'

She had been holding her breath, back rigid, and almost flinched as his finger touched her. She noticed there was a slight, attractive crookedness of a front tooth, a tiny mole beneath the left eye, a glistening droplet of moisture nestling in the hollow of his throat. She forced out a reply:

'My father was quite capable of assessing a ruined temple, or giving valuable information as to what happened thousands of years ago, but so far as I'm concerned, Professor Devlin, he was quite lousy when it came to the here and now and the living. I'm afraid his recommendation doesn't count much with me.'

He weighed her words carefully, the grey eyes never

leaving her face. With heavy patience he said:

'The sooner you accept the inevitable, the better it will be for you, and in the long run, for Ben too.'

Alex dropped her gaze, the tip of her tongue moistening her lips.

'I could make it very difficult for you.'

'Yes, you could, but somehow I don't think you will. The outcome will still be the same, but Ben will suffer . . . and therefore so will you.' He hesitated fractionally and then continued evenly: 'You'd better go to bed now, and think on it,' and he turned away and walked back to the desk and in a few seconds was immersed in his work.

Alex left him, a whisper of chiffon in the air, leaving the necklace of jasmine to wilt, discarded on the floor.

CHAPTER FOUR

'How long have you been in Thailand, Miss Templar?'

Alex's heart sank as she realised she was in for another inquisition. The coffee morning was already in progress when she had called unexpectedly on Melanie, and although she ought to have become used to being an object of curiosity and speculation she found that she was not.

Alex smiled, however, and replied: 'Nearly two months.'

'And how long do you intend to stay?' The speaker returned the smile, one meant to be encouraging, and four pairs of ears were pricked in readiness for the English girl's answer.

'My plans are flexible,' and Alex caught an amused look from Melanie, who had at that moment returned to the room carrying the tray of coffee things, sizing up the situation immediately.

'Now, Maudie, don't be wishing her gone before we've had the chance to enjoy her company. It's not often we have a pretty new face to look at—and do call her Alex, she won't mind, and it's more friendly.' She extended a plate, 'Cake or cookie, anyone?' adding to Alex: 'Where's Ben today?'

Alex replied with a chuckle: 'We decided to part company this morning. Ben felt he couldn't take another temple and I felt I couldn't take snakes.'

'He's gone to the Snake Farm, has he?' Melanie positioned herself next to her young friend and eyed her other guests speculatively. There was no real malice in any of them. The trouble was they didn't have enough to do. 'He'll find that real interesting, won't he, girls?'

A murmur of agreement went round the group, but Maudie was not one to give up easily.

'It certainly was a surprise to us all when we heard that Nick Devlin had visitors from England . . . and an even bigger one when we knew he was to be guardian to your brother.' Her New Jersey voice became all sympathy. 'Such a responsibility for Nick to take on! Especially without a wife to help him. But perhaps he intends doing something about that now?' and she paused, hopefully, but Alex remained silent, her face expressionless, and Maudie turned confidentially to her friends. 'I saw Suzanne yesterday,' she informed them, offering the information as a gift. Her too innocent eyes returned to Alex. 'Suzanne Miles . . . a great friend of Nick's.'

Alex said evenly: 'Yes, I know her.'

Maudie was disappointed and Alex mentally excused herself the lie. It was nearly the truth—she did know Suzanne, from a distance, and the memory of the attractive dark-haired girl coming up the theatre steps that fateful night in Singapore was as strong as ever. Melanie had supplied further information in the course of normal conversation.

Miss Suzanne Miles was twenty-eight, unmarried, highly intelligent, and worked at the American Embassy. Among the Western fraternity there was conjecture as to whether Miss Miles would eventually become Mrs Devlin. This, Melanie had declared, was derived by Suzanne being Nick's social partner more often than anyone else and not by anything more specific.

Where would Ben fit in if Suzanne and Nick

married? wondered Alex, sipping her coffee and allowing the conversation to go on around her. The thought was disturbing. From all she had heard Suzanne Miles didn't seem the type to welcome a ready-made family in the shape of an unknown eight-year-old English boy.

'I've always wondered about Nick and Varuni Khomang,' someone said, and this brought Alex abruptly from her reverie.

'What! Marry a Thai?' Maudie responded in a slightly shocked voice, and Melanie said brusquely:

'Why not? Varuni is a lovely girl.'

'Nick might find it politic to ally himself with one of the most influential families in Thailand,' another put in knowingly.

Alex escaped into the kitchen with the excuse of fetching more milk. She emptied it into a jug and stood, gazing with unseeing eyes out across the Carrs' swimming pool and tennis court, both deserted apart from a young Thai boy skimming the leaves from the surface of the water with a large net. Varuni and Nick? Yes, she could believe that to be possible, there was a gentleness about Nick where Varuni was concerned and as Melanie had said, she was a lovely person. But love? Here Alex frowned thoughtfully. She couldn't associate Nick with such a human frailty. His seemed to be a calculated, organised existence, self-sufficient and impenetrable. There was such a rock-like inner core of strength that was beginning to undermine her own reserves. Yes, she did believe it possible that Nick Devlin could marry for expediency. Would he do so for Ben?

She returned with the milk and found that the conversation had moved to recipes, and she made for the window seat and let it drift over her. All the talk about

Nick this morning had disturbed her and she decided, then and there, that she would have to have a serious discussion with him. It was no use just drifting from day to day like this. She felt anger with herself for allowing it to happen. Two months of sight-seeing and basking in the sun in idleness ... the lazy, happy-go-lucky Thai philosophy was enervating. It was very pleasant, of course, she'd be a fool if she didn't admit it, but it was getting them nowhere. At least, it was getting her nowhere, while she rather suspected that Nick was quite content to let things drift. The more she thought about it the more she realised how she was being manipulated. There he was, on the sidelines, watching and listening, a mine of information, a pleasant and most considerate host, arranging and guiding their leisure hours, joining them when his duties at the University allowed, drawing them into the company of his closest friends—lulling her into a false sense of security. For it couldn't last, could it?

When the others finally left and Melanie came back into the room from seeing them off, Alex asked slowly:

'Did you know Nick's wife, Mel?'

Melanie sat down and picked up her knitting. 'Martine? No. I don't know much about her either, I don't think anyone does, only that she and the boy died in a plane crash over in the States. His name was Christopher.' She gave a sympathetic sigh and began clicking the needles again. 'That's why, in a way, having Ben here must have brought back painful memories. Christopher would have been about your brother's age if he'd lived.'

Alex saw the Pontiac swing through the gates and turned from the window, snatching up her bag.

'Don't move, I can let myself out, Mel. Here's

Rachan come for me. Thanks for the coffee. We'll be seeing you all tomorrow, won't we?' She was at the front door now and heard Melanie's voice call after her:

'Yes, the boys are looking forward to it.'

Only when she had reached the enclosed verandah of the Carrs' Colonial-style house did Alex realise it was Nicholas and not Rachan outlined in the mesh-framed door. She pushed it open and let it bang behind her. At the noise Nicholas halted his journey from the car and looked up.

'Hello, Alex—that was quick.' He was dressed in the more formal clothes he used for the University and she could see that the back seat was strewn with books, papers and folders. There was sometimes a pupil, but today there was no one, not even Ben, and Alex's surprise changed to alarm as she ran down the steps to meet him.

'Nick! What are you doing here? Is something wrong with Ben?'

Dark brows rose. 'Why should you think that? It was more convenient for me to come for you first, that's all.' His voice had an edge of impatience. 'You're too sensitive where Ben's concerned, Alex. He's my responsibility now, let me do the worrying.'

The morning had been a trying one and she over-reacted.

'I suppose you mean I'm too protective! Knowing where he's gone it's hardly surprising I should worry ... snakes are dangerous, you know!' She wasn't proud of the sarcasm, but she couldn't help herself.

'Agreed, but Rachan is very capable and the security at the Snake Farm is excellent.' He looked at her keenly. 'You're quick to take offence today, aren't you?'

'I'm beginning to think I've not been quick enough. I don't want you to have the responsibility, or to do the worrying—can't you understand?'

There was silence while blue eyes glared defiantly into reflective grey ones.

'Something's upset you,' he said at last, and his eyes flicked to the house and back again. He put a hand beneath her arm to lead her to the car, but she shrugged it off. It was past noon and the heat on her flesh was fierce. Already Alex could feel drops of moisture running down her bare arms and legs. She was glad to reach the car which was parked in the shade of trees. Opening the door for her, Nicholas stated mildly: 'You ought to know by now that what Mel says . . .'

'Mel hasn't said anything,' Alex snapped . . . which wasn't quite true; innocently Mel had said quite a lot. He joined her, sliding his body behind the wheel, observing dryly:

'Someone has. Come on, Alexandra, tell me.'

She had noticed before that at certain times he made a distinction of calling her by her full name—and she resented the slow, drawling way he had of making it attractive. That was the whole trouble, she thought bitterly. If she didn't fight he'd make everything sound attractive.

'Perhaps I've just woken up to the fact that it's two months since we arrived and nothing's been settled yet!'

Nicholas started the car and drove out into the road.

'I thought you were enjoying yourself?'

'Of course I am, anyone would be,' she burst out impatiently. 'It's a wonderful experience being here, but you're trying to make out that everything's normal . . . that this is a holiday, and it isn't.'

'I thought we agreed to take things easy, allow Ben time to settle down . . .'

'You agreed.'

'. . . in a normal atmosphere . . .'

'It's a false situation,' broke in Alex again, her face setting obstinately. 'How can he settle down?'

'. . . and give you the chance to get to know me. Perhaps find that I'm not such an ogre as you were determined to expect.' He was all reasonableness and as inexorable as a steamroller, and just as flattening.

'It would take more than two months to do that,' she said grimly.

'Exactly.' The laconic answer wilfully misinterpreted her reply. 'Perhaps your letter this morning upset you?' The question showed polite concern, the look he gave with it was shrewd.

Alex set her mouth and didn't answer.

'It was from James Hicks, your solicitor, I believe? I too received a letter from him, telling me that he has now sold your father's house and contents. I can understand that this news would naturally cause you some distress.'

She raised her brows. 'Really?'

'The law demanded its sale, Alex, not I,' Nicholas pointed out curtly.

'Oh, well, it would have been too big and expensive to run anyway. We can find something smaller eventually, Ben and I.'

Nicholas gave a short laugh. 'You're certainly a fighter, Alex, I can say that for you!' and Alex swung round in the seat and directed herself to his profile.

'And you're a clever man, Nick Devlin, and it would be silly of me to underestimate you. You find yourself in a situation where you're landed with a ward you don't want and his sister who's not prepared to hand him over to a total stranger. So what do you do? Confuse the issue with good manners, good living and the fascinating lure of the East. Well, it's not working.'

The car hummed along smoothly, the air-conditioning a blessing on her fiery cheeks. As Nicholas swung into Rama IV Road, easing into the four-lane snarl-up towards the Snake Farm entrance, he commented coolly:

'You're wrong on two counts. I do want Ben, and don't be so sure of the good manners, Alexandra,' and conversation between them ceased.

The evening meal of the same day was made lively by Ben's visit to the Snake Farm. The boy was full of enthusiasm and for his age he appeared to have taken in much of what he had seen, and what he didn't know Nicholas was able to tell him.

Alex sat quietly, with little appetite. She felt confused, depressed and uneasy. She had spent the afternoon with Ben by the pool, her thoughts returning again and again to her outburst earlier. If only she had remained as calm as Nick! Somehow his composure made her worse—and what had she achieved? Nothing. When he had walked into the apartment this evening and greeted her the whole episode might never have happened.

She stabbed uninterestedly at the food on her plate and then abandoned all pretence at eating. She felt a bit queasy and wondered whether she'd had too much sun ... or perhaps it was just nerves! Giving an inward sigh, she reflected that if it hadn't been for the gossip about Nick that morning the outburst wouldn't have occurred. They would probably have discussed the plans for their weekend trip with the Khomangs and the Carrs to the Elephant Round-up Show at Surin and Nick might have suggested a quick game of squash at the International Sports Club. As it was he went off alone, and it was more than likely he found a more than adequate partner in a lanky Australian girl called Dorothy who had a predatory gleam in her eye where the Professor was concerned. And what about Sally, the American attaché's daughter, on a visit from the States? As Melanie had said at their first meeting, Nicholas Devlin was a popular man.

She eyed him down the length of the table and envied him his appetite. Eating steadily, Nicholas nodded every now and then, his eyes flicking from his plate to Ben's face, sometimes listening, sometimes answering a question as he did now.

'I suppose the most deadly snake is the cobra,' he replied, signalling to Malee to remove the dishes.

'I saw a cobra,' Ben informed them with satisfaction. 'Did you know they can swim, Alex? And they have to be force-fed by the keepers.'

'It sounds cruel,' Nicholas intervened, 'but they won't eat in captivity. And the Institute provides a real need in the manufacture of vaccines and sera—they export to quite a few countries.'

'Really?' responded Alex, valiantly trying to show some interest and her brother nodded, beaming. She smiled back, a rush of love sweeping over her. Ben's hair, if anything, was even whiter, bleached by the sun's rays. Malee took a zealous care over their clothes which needed to be constantly changed because of the heat, and his blue shirt seemed to make his eyes bluer than ever. She was sure he was filling out a little, although that was probably wishful thinking. He certainly looked well. 'Have you been wearing your hat, Ben?' she asked, referring to the jaunty denim hooked on the back of his chair. 'You're beginning to look like a lobster.'

Ben grinned: 'So are you.'

Alex pulled a face. 'I know, and I've been so careful, too.'

'I'm afraid yesterday was the trouble,' Nicholas stated, looking them both over critically, and referring to their day's outing by boat along the klongs. 'Being out all day in the fresh air, even in the shade, is difficult, with skins as fair as yours. I have some good cream that should help to lessen the burning and you must cover up tomorrow—wear long sleeves and trousers, both of you.'

'What will it be like at Surin, Nick?' Ben asked, and Nicholas replied with a grin:

'Rather like an elephant gymkhana.'

Malee came in from the kitchen, a wide smile on her face, carrying a dish which she set with aplomb in the middle of the table. Nicholas raised his brows and looked from his maid to Alex, who coloured slightly.

'It's one of Alex's pies,' Ben declared, his voice showing his approval, and Alex murmured:

'I don't know what it'll be like. English fruit I can cope with, but I'm not so sure about Thai.'

'Missy make good,' Malee announced firmly, handing Alex the knife and Nicholas held out his plate, saying quizzically to Ben:

'Shall we try it, Ben?' adding blandly, 'They do say that the way to a man's heart is his stomach.'

Alex, busily transferring a portion on to his plate, paused, meeting his eyes. Oh, yes, the man had charm all right, and she found herself responding to the teasing smile by saying lightly:

'Aren't you taking rather a risk, then?'

'I think my heart and my stomach are strong

enough,' he replied rather dryly, and for once Alex was in total agreement. The pie was demolished with gratifying speed and when Malee brought in the coffee Ben returned to the subject nearest to his heart at the moment.

'Have you seen a cobra, Nick? A wild one?'

'I have, but there was little danger. I was on the lookout just in case and wore protective boots.' Nicholas pushed back his chair, settling into a more relaxed position. 'Snakes are not naturally aggressive and will only bite when provoked.'

'How nice to know,' murmured Alex. 'I must remember not to provoke.'

'King Cobra are bigger, of course. They can reach up to twenty feet.' Nicholas offered this choice piece of information as he set up the lighting of a cigar.

'Golly!' Ben's eyes were wide. 'Rachan says he's seen plenty of snakes here in Bangkok.'

Alex stared at her brother aghast and he nodded. 'They live in the canals and gardens and eat rats and other snakes.'

Seeing her look of horror, Nicholas said kindly: 'Snakes sleep during the day and so long as you keep away from long undergrowth and trees at night you'll be all right.'

'Thank you. What a useful piece of information,' Alex said with heavy calm. 'And to think that I was scared of the gecko! Why, they're the darlingest of creatures.'

'There's a book on snakes on the shelf over there, Ben. The large red one, second up. You may take it to look at if you like.'

'After you've washed your hands,' added Alex pointedly, and Ben, face alight with pleasure, marvelled:

'May I, Nick? Thank you!' and intoning a 'Please may I leave the table,' he disappeared rapidly in the direction of the bathroom without waiting for a reply.

'There are better subjects for conversation at the table than reptiles,' Nicholas conceded, amusement tinging his voice. 'Do they really concern you?'

'Oh, no, not when I'm sitting six floors up in a modern apartment building,' Alex told him graciously as she poured out the coffee, and thought that she ought to try and make him laugh more often. 'What time shall we be starting tomorrow?'

'As near seven as we can make it,' Nicholas replied, taking the cup she was offering. 'I want to get through the city before the traffic builds up. We're staying over-night at a place called Khorat and will make a start for Surin the following morning around four-thirty.' He saw Alex's look of surprise and explained: 'Khorat is some hundred and sixty miles from Bangkok and Surin another hundred on top of that. The Show begins at eight-thirty to take advantage of the coolest part of the day, so we're bound to break the journey.'

'In that case I'll make sure Ben's in bed early,' and giving a small yawn, Alex laughed and said: 'Me too.'

Nicholas drained his coffee and rising and making for his room, reminded her about the sunburn cream. He returned a few moments later with it in his hand, and without waiting for her to demur began to smooth the cream across her shoulders and upper back, his hands working quickly and efficiently.

'Put some more on just before you go to bed,' he advised, handing her the tube, and indicating her hair which was in a loose twist on the top of her head, remarked: 'The sun's making your hair quite streaky,' before walking back to his room. Some moments later there was the sound of running water from the main bathroom.

Alex stood for a few seconds turning the tube over in her fingers. Where he had touched her the skin glowed. Absently she attended to her arms, saying a goodnight to Malee as she made for her own quarters. Ben appeared, duly washed, and submitted to being creamed, giggling when Alex dabbed a blob on the end of his nose. On her words 'you'll do' he hastened to the bookshelf and reached eagerly for the snake book.

Alex began to say casually: 'Can you manage ...?' when the heavy book slipped out of Ben's hands and crashed on to the cupboard below, clipping the edge of a small antique bowl. Alex sprang forward, shouting: 'Ben, look out!' but she was too far away and they both watched in horror as the bowl started its journey in slow motion across the polished surface of the wood. It came to a jarring halt against the statue of the bronze Buddha, the force of impact toppling the bowl and causing the lid to fall off, pivoting round and round until it gradually lost momentum and lay still, barely an inch from the edge.

There was a stunned silence for a moment as brother and sister stared at each other in acute dismay and Alex, hands to mouth, let out a long-held breath.

'Oh, Ben! If it had broken!' She saw his eyes move past her and swinging round she saw Nicholas standing in the doorway of his bathroom, the remains of shaving cream on his face. He had stripped off to the waist and a towel hung round his neck.

'What happened?' he asked, moving across to join them, still wiping his chin with the end of the towel.

'I dropped the book,' whispered Ben, his face beginning to crumple. 'I'm sorry.'

Alex stepped quickly to him, placing her hands protectingly on his shoulders, her face as white as her brother's as they stood together facing his guardian.

Nicholas assessed the situation and then picked up the book, handing it to Ben. 'No harm done,' he said briefly, and ruffling the boy's hair gave him a little push. 'Off you go.'

With a quick, upward look of relief at his sister, Ben rushed to his room. Alex stood rigid as Nicholas replaced the lid and put the bowl back in place. When he began to walk back towards the bathroom she said in amazement:

'Aren't you going to say anything?'

He turned, brows raised. 'What do you want me to say?'

She stared at him helplessly and shook her head. 'I don't know.'

Nicholas retraced his steps. 'Perhaps I should alter that to what did you expect me to say?'

Alex searched his face, but it told her nothing. Her own feelings were in a tumult and she understood neither herself nor Nicholas.

'Oh, don't you see how impossible it all is?' she broke out passionately. 'What would you have done if your precious bowl had broken?'

Nicholas shrugged. 'Raised the roof . . . given him a few hard minutes of my tongue,' His gaze went round the room. 'I suppose I could put everything away, but I believe things of beauty should be seen and admired even if they sometimes get broken.'

'That's easy enough to say—it didn't break,' accused Alex.

He picked the bowl up, turning it thoughtfully round in his hand. 'It's rather a good piece . . . seven-teenth-century, or thereabouts. Can you see it's made up of five colours? Bencharong means just that—five colours . . . made in China following Thai designs.'

His mouth twisted and his voice hardened. 'No, it didn't break. Do you want me to prove myself? I can, quite easily,' and he held the bowl poised above the floor and in a flash, Alex shot out her hands and imprisoned the bowl, still in his palm.

'Nick, don't!' Contact was instant, vibrant and alive. 'Oh, how absurd you are!' she exclaimed despairingly. 'Please don't, I believe you.'

It seemed an age that they stood there, hands joined, Alex staring up into his face which was dark and forbidding, Nicholas frowning down at the slender, pale hands covering his own. She felt his fingers stir and she released him, her eyes dropping to the delicate porcelain now balanced in his opened palm. She took it from him, hands trembling slightly, and moved to the cupboard, restoring it gently to its original position. A fine piece . . . yes, indeed, it was, and she leaned against the cupboard, her back still turned, imagining all those tiny colours scattered on the floor. Nicholas began to speak and there was a decided edge to his voice.

'It could easily have been you or me. Even adults are known to be careless. Please don't insult me by thinking I put possessions before people.'

It seemed important to justify herself, and Alex swung round, eyes wide and troubled. 'I . . . I'm sorry. Forgive me, please. I've been brought up in a house where possessions are worshipped behind glass doors.' The words were almost inaudible. She was acutely aware of the faint perfume of shaving cream juxtaposed with the masculine smell of his body . . . the texture of the white, fluffy towel as it lay against the deeply tanned, moist curve of shoulder and upper arm. Alex shivered and felt cold, even as her skin burned with a feverish heat. She forced herself to con-

centrate. She mustn't do anything silly like bursting
into tears, for that would mean being comforted and
she might be tempted to give up the fight ... tempted
to take the pleasure of being held by someone strong
and capable, and not to have to worry any more. Her
resolve was not strengthened by hearing him give a
deep sigh before saying gently:

'What a funny, intense thing you are, Alexandra
Jane,' and when she didn't answer, couldn't answer,
Nicholas scolded lightly: 'I've told you not to worry.
Why can't you trust me?' He had asked that of her
before. She was torn in two, desperately wanting to
and yet not daring to take the chance. She forced herself to speak.

'I've told you, I could never trust my father ... why
should you expect me to trust you? A stranger?' The
words came out dully. She wouldn't look at him.

'So it's still war, is it, Alex? Ah, well ...' and he
turned to leave her.

'At Mel's today there were visitors.' The tone more
than the information stopped his stride. 'Taking coffee
and biscuits. American friends of Mel's. They all
wanted to know if you were going to marry Suzanne
Miles.'

Nicholas pivoted round. 'Really? What did you tell
them?'

This was better. The gentleness had gone. She
couldn't stand too much of the gentleness. Her nerve
very nearly faltered at the steel grey of his eyes.

'I couldn't tell them anything, could I? I mean, I
don't know Suzanne. Does she like eight-year-old
boys?'

'I have no idea,' Nicholas stated repressively, and
made for the bathroom, broad back set rigid.

'Well, you'd better find out before you ask her,

hadn't you!' As the defiant order whipped coldly after him, Nicholas halted abruptly and turned, looking across the room consideringly at the girl, aware that every tense bone in her body shouted a challenge.

'You're trying to provoke me, Alex. Be careful . . . one day you might succeed,' and then he disappeared purposefully into the bathroom and closed the door on her.

When he returned some time later Alex was curled up in a chair pretending to be reading, so absorbed in the book that she was unaware of his presence. They both knew it was a sham.

Nicholas tossed the car keys in his hands, looking down at the crown of her fair head, the soft curve of hair hiding her face.

'I'm going out now, Alex. I won't be late. You'll be all right?'

She allowed herself a sweeping upward glance. 'Of course. You needn't worry about us, we're quite used to being on our own, you know,' and she returned her eyes to the print in total absorption. A measured pause and then she heard him walk to the door.

'I'll say goodnight, in case you're in bed when I get back,' he responded, quite unruffled.

Alex murmured a reply, deep in the book, and heard the door close. For a long while she stared at the jumbled words blurred with unshed tears. Closing the book with careful precision, she leaned back against the cushions and closed her eyes.

What on earth's the matter with you, Alex Templar? she demanded of herself. Just what do you think you achieved by all that? A tear crept out between her lashes and rolled down her cheek and she brushed it angrily away. She wasn't going to cry over Nick Devlin, damn him!

So it's still war, is it, Alex? His words rang in her ears. Yes, it was! It had to be! She thrust herself impatiently from the chair and went to stare out of the window, the lights of the city spread out before her, twinkling in the darkness.

She wondered where he was going and who warranted the smart navy blazer, and then the telephone began to ring. There was a pause after she said the number.

'Is Nicky in, please? Tell him it's Suzanne.' The voice was markedly American and attractively husky.

'I'm sorry, he's just left. Can I take a message?' Alex asked, all politeness.

'Oh, no, that won't be necessary. I thought I could catch him, but it's not too important. I'll be seeing him tonight, anyway. Thanks all the same.'

There was a click. Alex replaced the telephone very gently. Well, now she knew—and knowing didn't help.

'Nicky', indeed!

CHAPTER FIVE

It was typical of Nicholas that they should be four minutes within their deadline for departure. With the weekend luggage stored in the boot they set off with Rachan driving and inside the hour had left the city behind.

It was left to Nicholas and Ben to make any conversation, for Alex was feeling decidedly below par. It had taken her a long time before she had fallen asleep, too much was going on inside her head. As late as it was, when she finally did drop off, Nicholas had not returned. She had woken that morning lethargic, still feeling slightly nauseous and with an aching head. Her lack of breakfast, apart from coffee, went unnoticed in the hustle of leaving and if her lack of talk didn't, Nicholas would probably put it down to their fight the night before.

Just outside the city they passed the saffron-robed figures of two shaven-headed monks, each carrying a bowl, and Ben, sitting in the back with Alex, leaned forward and asked:

'Are they begging, Nick?'

His guardian shook his head, half turning to reply:

'By no means . . . they're receiving alms. The Thai people believe that they gain merit by giving food to the monks. Merit is thought to purify the mind and wash away greed and hatred. By doing good deeds they're making a spiritual investment, a reward if you like, for a better life after rebirth.' He glanced at Alex, lying back in the corner, eyes closed, and then returned to Ben. 'Buddha isn't a god. The Thais don't worship as such, rather they consider him to be a teacher, and try to follow his teachings. They believe each man is responsible for his own destiny, and try to avoid all evil and live a good life.'

Each man is responsible for his own destiny. An interesting philosophy, Alex reflected as she listened to his voice, and wondered how much truth there was in it. Her lashes lifted slightly until she could see Nicholas and Ben. She recalled Melanie's words that Nicholas's son would be Ben's age now had he lived and the unspoken follow-up that Ben could take his place. Was that the main reason why Nicholas had taken on the guardianship? How complicated things were getting! Nothing was as it seemed.

'What are those decorated bird tables with roofs on?' Ben was asking, pointing a finger. 'There's one.'

She saw Nicholas smile, pitting his leathery face with deep grooves, his teeth white against the tan.

'That's a dwelling place for the guardian spirit— every house has one. The Thais believe in spirits, almost one for every occasion. Isn't that so, Rachan?' and he turned to his driver, who nodded happily in agreement. Back again to Ben, Nicholas went on: 'If you look closely you'll be able to see that gifts have been left there—flowers, joss-sticks or a lighted candle. A visitor always pays his respects to the house-spirit and requests permission to sleep and seek protection.' His voice deepened with amusement. 'Sometimes the spirit says the time isn't an auspicious one for working and then everyone downs tools. Thailand has proved too much for many a Western foreman, eh, Rachan?' and the Thai grinned broadly.

The road to Khorat was a good one by Thai standards. The flat countryside around the Bangkok Basin

was soon left behind and they began to climb slowly
through a range of hills towards the Khorat Plateau,
the road curving to give magnificent views of thick
forests, a gleaming lake, the hint of a waterfall sparkling through tangled greenery and tall clusters of
waving bamboo. They stopped a couple of times to
stretch their legs and again to eat a midday meal at a
roadside café attached to a filling station, the only hab-
itation, apart from an occasional farm, they had passed
for miles.

Alex surreptitiously took two pills for her head and
toyed with the food. As soon as she was able she wandered outside and sat under some trees, fanning herself gently with her sunhat. She let her mind wander
back to the previous evening when she had gone in to
Ben to say goodnight. She had found him immersed in
the snake book but quite ready to put it on one side
and snuggle down the bedclothes with a yawn. His
face glowed up at her from the pillow, the bleached
fairness of his hair and the scrubbed, rosy cheeks of
his sweet face giving him an angelic look that tugged at
her heart. How difficult it was to know what was the
best thing for Ben. She had come to Thailand with no
doubts, but they were beginning to creep in, unbidden
and unwanted.

'How are you liking it here, Ben, with Nick?' she
asked casually, sitting on the side of the bed as she
always did for their nightly chat.

'It's great! I can't wait for tomorrow. Just think,
Alex, over two hundred elephants, Nick says, and real,
working ones too! Do you think I shall be able to ride
one?'

Alex was becoming used to the 'Nick says' these
days.

'I've no idea, darling, you'll have to wait and see.'

She paused. 'And Nick? Do you like Nick, Ben?'

'Oh, yes, Nick's all right, isn't he?' Ben sat up and leaned on an elbow, his voice slightly sheepish. 'I was scared of coming, Alex, weren't you? But it's like you said—Father wouldn't have chosen someone horrible, would he?' He lay back with a bounce while Alex reflected ruefully that she had done a better job than she had thought on their father's image. 'Golly, Nick knows a lot! and I can talk to him and he always listens. I thought he'd be really angry tonight when I dropped that book and nearly broke his bowl, but he wasn't, was he? He understood it was an accident.' He smiled. 'You like him too, don't you, Alex?'

Alex jumped a little guiltily at the question and stammered:

'What? Oh, yes . . . yes, of course. But Ben, how do you feel now, about staying with Nick, I mean?'

'I don't mind. I think I'm quite looking forward to school—Bud and Johnnie talk about it all the time. They say Nick's finishing at the University this term and they heard their mum say she thought he'd go up North to write his book. Just think, Alex, he's got the King's permission to write it—all about the people and the history and things.'

Alex turned a startled face. 'Leaving the University?' she echoed, her voice high with surprise.

'Yes . . . and now he's got Father's book to put together too. It's in a bit of a muddle, but Nick will sort it out, and you'll be able to help him, Alex, won't you?' he pronounced with supreme confidence. 'And if he . . .'

'But Ben, I might not be here.' There, the words were out.

He wrinkled his nose. 'Why not?'

'Well, I can't stay here for ever . . .'

'Why not? If Nick will let you?' An anxious note
was beginning to creep into his voice and Alex went
on lightly:

'But I'm not part of Nick's life, dear. You are, because of Father's will . . . he made Nick your guardian
and . . .'

'Nick promised me you could stay!' Ben said
gruffly, turning his face to the wall, and Alex bit her
lip, fighting for the right words.

'He didn't exactly promise I could stay for ever,' she
reminded him carefully. 'Not for ever, Ben, just until
you settled in. You say you like it here, and you've
made friends and you get on well with Nick . . .'

'I'm not staying without you.' His voice was
muffled in the pillow and Alex began to talk quickly,
reassuringly.

'Listen to me, Ben. I think Nick will be a good
guardian for you. We would have been fine on our
own, but Father thought it better for Nick to look
after us . . . and who knows, maybe he's right. Now
I'm sure I'll be able to stay on here for a while yet, but
Nick may have plans that don't include me,' and time
would tell whether Ben would need to be told the possibility of Nicholas marrying, she thought, pushing
the idea violently on one side. Ben turned his head on
the pillow and she could see tears on his cheeks.

'Bud says Nick will probably send me back to England for my senior schooling anyway. Most folk do.
And then you could come back with me, Alex.'

Alex felt a stab of forlorn amusement as she realised
that for Ben it was a foregone conclusion that she
would be happy to fit her life into his plans . . . and
who could blame him? All his short life she had done
just that, and it wasn't likely she was going to stop
now, was it?

'If Nick won't let you stay then I won't either ...
I'll run away!' Ben's voice now had a stubborn edge to
it and Alex hid a sigh. Now wasn't the time to point
out that unfortunately neither of them had any say in
the matter. She brightened her voice purposefully.

'It doesn't mean that I shall go away altogether,
Ben. I shall try and get a job. Anyway, we needn't
make any decisions now, darling. It's getting late and
we have to be up early tomorrow. Don't worry about a
thing. Everything will turn out all right, you'll see,'
and on that confident note she had smoothed back his
hair and kissed him goodnight. She had returned to
her own room knowing just how hollow that confidence was ... knowing that if Nicholas decided to
marry again, and with Ben in mind she didn't agree
his choice, there was nothing she could do other than
stir Ben up. And she couldn't do that. As Nicholas had
once said, she couldn't win at Ben's expense.

A shadow crossed her face and she opened her eyes
to find Nicholas looking down at her, a frown on his
face.

'We're ready to go,' he stated briefly.

Alex rose, brushing down her coffee-coloured trousers and tucking in the cream blouse before following
him to the car.

As he waited by the open door, Nicholas stayed her
entrance by a hand on her shoulder and she looked up
enquiringly.

'Are you feeling all right?' he asked, and she replied
that she was, sliding into the seat without looking at
him again.

They arrived at the old fortress town of Khorat in
the early afternoon to find the others already there.
The Khomangs were with a doctor friend, who was
referred to as Somchai. Varuni looked cool and beauti-

ful in a deep orchid-pink Oriental trouser and top, her long black hair caught back with a spray of orchids the same colour. Melanie and Warren had only just arrived with their two boys and a surprise guest, Suzanne Miles.

Alex studied the American girl carefully and after half an hour in her company could understand why Nicholas was attracted. She was beautiful, intelligent, witty and self-assured—the kind of female, Alex decided with resignation, as they made their way to the rooms allocated in the hotel, that made her feel feeble-minded at the best of times, and today was definitely not one of her best. Suzanne still managed to look as stunning in a cream outfit that was as fresh and clean as when she first put it on. Her hair had bounce and spring, her eyes glowed and her teeth sparkled in an ever-ready smile. She made Alex weary to look at her.

It was decided not to waste any of the day, although all Alex wanted to do was to collapse into her bed, and after wandering round the town for a while they drove the few miles to the ruined temple of Phimai, one of the oldest historical remains in the area.

Nicholas was a good man to have as a guide and discoursed authoritatively and with interest as they walked round. After some time Alex dropped behind and found a spot of cool shade beyond one of the ruined archways. She could hear voices coming intermittently across the clear air and the shouts of the boys as they raced around getting rid of their surplus energy. It was pleasant sitting there, not having to make an effort.

When a shadow fell across the sunlit steps Alex realised her privacy was being invaded and looked up with some misgivings to see Suzanne, her camera swinging from her hand, the other removing large dark glasses. The hazel eyes were clear and direct.

'So this is where you're hiding yourself,' she observed, voice cool. 'We've been taking photographs so you'll be able to show the folks back home in England when you go,' and she stepped lightly down the steps to join Alex in her hideout.

'How kind of you,' Alex replied dryly. There was to be no beating about the bush.

Placing a sandalled foot on one of the fallen stones, Suzanne rested an arm across one knee and with the other hand bent down to rub a scuff mark from the leather with the tip of a finger. 'When do you reckon on going back? I mean, you won't want to be here too long, will you? If you've left your home and job ...' and her voice trailed, leaving the question hanging in the air. Alex replied obligingly:

'The house has been sold and my job wasn't an important one, like yours. You'll have to ask Nicholas about my return.'

Suzanne straightened and eyed her carefully. 'Hmm ... yes, well, Nicky has some cute ideas, hasn't he? He also has a strong sense of duty—which is my tough luck, though I guess I wouldn't love him any different. I hadn't bargained for an eight-year-old ward, I must admit, and I needn't tell you that I'm doing all I can to persuade Nicky to let your brother go back with you—in a subtle way, of course. If I can't persuade him I can still cope. After all, Ben will be away at school for most of the time and I can get on with him if I put my mind to it.'

'You're very frank.'

Suzanne shrugged. 'Why not? I'm a great believer in putting my cards on the table.' She tilted her head consideringly. 'I can't make you out. I guess you're on the level.'

Alex raised her brows. 'Why shouldn't I be?'

'Singapore is a trifle hard to swallow, honey.'

Alex felt the blood rush to her face. Nicholas had told her about Singapore!

'You aren't Nicky's type, that's something.'

'You must be relieved.' Alex rose to her feet. 'I think that's the others calling us. Shall we go?'

Why she was so angry Alex didn't know, but she was. How dared he tell Suzanne about Singapore! She returned to Khorat in Kasem's care, barely recognising Nicholas's existence. It didn't help that with Suzanne hanging on his arm he was totally unaware of the fact. Back once more in the private luxury of her own room Alex threw herself into bed and in two seconds was asleep.

A knocking on the communicating door woke her with a start. Confused at first, she soon realised where she was and slipping on her robe went over and stood by it, saying a hesitant: 'Yes?'

'Alex, I want to speak to you.'

She turned the key and opened the door and Nicholas stepped in, dressed ready for dinner. His room was bright with light behind him and she blinked uncertainly, turning away.

'I'm sorry, Nick, am I late? Is it time to go down to eat?'

'No, you're not late. I was concerned when I could hear no movement from your room.' He drew his wrist up and glanced briefly at his watch. 'I'll call you in twenty minutes and we can go down together.' He looked round the room. 'Is everything all right?'

'Yes, thank you,' Alex replied automatically, and giving her another searching look Nicholas went back to his room and she closed the door. She stood for a moment looking at the key, hearing Nicholas moving about the other side, and then left it. She telephoned through to Ben who was sharing a room further along the corridor with Bud and Johnnie to check that he was getting ready, and then showered and dressed, taking two more pills. It was obvious she was sickening for something, but with a bit of luck she might be able to shake it off without anyone guessing. She had no intention of being a drag on the weekend's entertainment.

By the time Nicholas knocked again she was just putting the finishing touches to her face. Calling out that she would be ready in a minute, she stood back and looked herself over critically in the mirror. Two bright spots of colour burned on her cheeks and she hurried to dab some powder over the tell-tale flush. She smoothed down the skirt of the silk jersey dress she had chosen to wear, deciding that the deep sea-green shade was one of her favourite colours, and then catching up a soft wool stole in case she had another attack of the shivers she opened the communicating door.

Nicholas was leafing through a folder of papers which he put down at her entrance and in silence they left his room and walked down the corridor towards the lift.

Did he know how women looked at him? Alex wondered, observing the side glances from two of her fellow passengers. Yes, of course he did, she decided, but he gave no sign and there was a reserve, an indefinable edge of steel beneath the easy manner that made women a little frightened of him. Perhaps that was part of his charm? Another was the easy way he wore his clothes, whether they were khakis or evening gear, as now. As the doors opened and they stepped out into the hotel lounge some impulse made her ask:

'Did your suit ever recover from the devastation of Singapore?'

'Oh, yes, it takes more than a ducking to keep a good suit down. The memories don't fit so good, though,' and on that dry note he took her arm and led her into the dining room. Only then did Alex remember that she had a grievance against him regarding Singapore.

It was a gay, convivial party that seated themselves at a large table decorated with candles and flowers on the hotel's roof-top dining room. Kasem was in charge of all the arrangements and the management welcomed the patronage of such an illustrious family with wide smiles and a nice sense of attention. Alex found herself seated next to the undemanding Warren with Ben on her other side. When the meal was over the three boys were excused, with strict orders to go to bed, and the adults continued to chat and smoke until the time was noticed and their early start the following day recalled. Before the party broke up, Kasem rose to his feet and addressing a blushing Varuni made it known that his sister had just become engaged to his good friend Somchai. Amidst general congratulations Alex looked for surprise or even distress on Nicholas's face, but could find none, only quiet satisfaction, as though the news was already known to him.

It was still dark when they left Khorat the following morning, the sun just beginning to come up over the horizon. Alex made a small murmur of appreciation as the bright orange and yellow rays streaked across the sky and landscape. Ben was lying across her lap, asleep again, and Nicholas, talking in a low voice to Rachan about their plans for the day, caught the sound and glanced back for a moment and then followed her gaze before continuing his conversation.

By five-thirty housewives living in the villages and towns they passed through were making their way to market and the farmers were walking their water buffaloes along the road-edge to the rice fields. It was light and still cool. By half-past seven the sun was well up and gaining strength.

The Elephant Round-up Show at Surin was a yearly event to which Thai families for miles around brought themselves with great enthusiasm. Lately it had become a tourist attraction, hence the Western newspaper reporters and photographers lining the field, and the running commentary relayed over the Tannoy in English, French, German as well as Thai. The huge gathering of spectators made parking difficult, and only by clinging to each other and keeping close could the Khomang party move to their seats without becoming separated. The huge grandstand in which they were sitting had a fixed roof awning, but it was still necessary to wear sunhats and dark glasses as protection from the fierce heat of the sun's rays.

For three and a half hours Alex went through the motions with a zombie-like determination. She laughed and clapped when the elephants played football and ran races, she cheered when they won the tug o'-war, listened to the singing from the tribal dancers and watched a mock battle between two 'armies' in full ceremonial battle dress of days gone by, looking like extras from a Hollywood movie.

At last the Show was over. Kasem announced that they would travel to Khorat for lunch, although the majority of the spectators would stay all day, for there was a carnival air about the place with stalls cooking delicious food and selling all kinds of wares to tempt the passer-by. While Alex helped Varuni to pack away the picnic basket which had contained their breakfast of barbecued beef, chicken legs and sticky rice, Ben wriggled his way over and told her he was going to look at the elephants and see if he could get a ride.

She absently watched him worm his way along the row of seats, coming to the conclusion that she was going to have to own up to feeling ill. Whatever plans had been made for the rest of the weekend she would have to opt out ... the persistent headache thumping away like a hammer and the ominous stomach pains that were gripping her, causing her to break out into a cold sweat, were becoming too bad to ignore.

On Nicholas's advice to keep together they began to wend their way along the grandstand, treading carefully down the steep steps. How it happened Alex did not know: one minute the others were ahead and the next she was swallowed up in the crowd alone. She couldn't believe it at first. In vain she looked for Warren's red hair or Nicholas's distinctive height, but whichever way she looked she saw a sea of strangers. Thinking that they must have turned off the main track without her noticing, she retraced her steps, this time with difficulty as she was going against the flow of the crowd. Her eyes eagerly sought a familiar face, but with sinking heart she could see none of her friends. The feeling of dismay was more for the trouble and anxiety she would cause when her absence was discovered than on her own account, but she thought with longing of her bed back at Khorat and wiping the perspiration from her face she gazed round the stadium trying to assess the direction of the car-park.

Suddenly the holiday atmosphere changed drastically from one of enjoyment to one of panic and hysteria. Somewhere ahead there was a disturbance with shouting and screaming. People began to push and

shove, all round her voices were raised in bewilderment and Alex found herself trapped in a seething
mass of bodies made worse by her not knowing what
was happening.

A vision of Ben trapped in a similar situation struck
her, and she could have wept at her stupidity in allowing him to go off to see the elephants. It was more
important than ever to find the others, but she found
she was having difficulty in keeping on her feet and
she had no control over her direction, being swept
along on a hysterical frantic tide of humanity.

'What is it? What's the matter?' she cried to those
nearest to her, and finally, understanding the question,
someone shouted that one of the elephants had broken
loose and was on the rampage.

Alex began to feel frantic, searching wildly round
looking for Ben, knowing it was hopeless—even if she
saw him she was helpless.

Whistles were now joining in with the other noises
and coming closer the awful sound of an elephant
trumpeting. She caught a glimpse of terrified people
clinging to a seating contraption strapped to one of the
elephant's back as it ploughed by, scattering the crowd
either side. Straining on tiptoes, she cast her eyes
wildly after it, trying to see if Ben was part of that
terrible scene.

And then she saw Nicholas. She could hardly believe her eyes as he made his way steadily towards her,
a set, grim look on his face.

When he was in hailing distance she cried: 'Nick!
Ben! Where's Ben?' and then his hands were upon her
and she was dependent completely on his strength.
'Nick, Ben was going for a ride!' she gasped, her body
shaken by trembling. 'Don't you understand? He
might be hurt! I must go and see ...' and she

struggled in his arms, fighting ineffectually to set herself free.

'Alex! Ben's safe.'

She stared up at him, blankly, white-faced and bedraggled. 'Safe?' she echoed, hardly daring to believe him.

'Yes, safe, you crazy woman!'

'Thank God!' she sobbed in relief. 'I thought . . . he said . . .'

Nicholas was half carrying her by now, his body protecting her from the crush. 'Ben's got more sense to listen to what I say!' he told her grimly. 'What the hell do you think you're doing, getting yourself lost like this?' The grey eyes glared down at her and she said weakly:

'I'm so sorry, Nick . . .' and gave up the attempt to say any more. Now was neither the time nor the place. All she could feel was an overwhelming thankfulness that her brother was safe, and she was quite willing to accept all the wrath that Nicholas intended to bestow on her.

The wrath, when it came, was not from Nicholas but from a falling piece of timber. They were passing a row of stalls which had been half demolished during the rampage and one of them crashed its way to the ground, knocking Alex unconscious in one fell swoop.

When she woke it was quiet. The room she was in was bare of only essentials and primitive in style. She moved tentatively, wriggling fingers and toes, coming to the conclusion that nothing was broken but her head, which was bandaged. Varuni was sleeping on the other pallet on the floor and through the cracks in the shutters Alex could tell it was night. She wished she could remember what had happened, but couldn't, and in a few moments she was asleep. She woke again and could remember being carried, her head against a hard shoulder. Gone were the harsh noises and in their place were hushed voices and gentle hands.

When Alex woke to total consciousness the shutters were half open and the sun shining beyond. There was the sound of a child's voice floating on the air and movement below. She realised that she was in a Thai house, on stilts, and the pallet on which Varuni had been sleeping was now empty.

Almost as if she knew herself to be in Alex's thoughts, Varuni came into the room, a smile coming to her face when she saw that Alex was awake.

'Alex, my dear friend! How are you feeling this morning?'

Alex returned her smile weakly, grimacing as she moved her head to greet Varuni.

'Ouch . . . I'm all right if I keep still!' She gazed up at the Thai girl anxiously. 'Varuni, what a nuisance I've been! Where are we? And where are the others? Is Ben all right?'

'So many questions! All will be answered presently. Now do not tax yourself, Alex,' and Varuni knelt by the bed and busied herself with a tray nearby. 'First you must take the medicine that Somchai has left for you.' She waited while this was achieved and continued calmly: 'We are in a farmhouse not far from Surin. We could not take you back to Khorat, it was too far, and Kasem remembered an old family friend who farmed in the district.' She began to wash her patient's hands and face with the aid of a cloth dipped in an earthenware bowl filled with refreshing cool water.

Alex felt tears prick her eyes. 'How kind of your friends to take me in . . . and you, Varuni, to stay. I can't thank you enough.'

'You must not try,' Varuni scolded her gently.

'Do tell me what happened, Varuni,' begged Alex. 'Did anyone else get hurt? What made the elephant act that way?' She hesitated. 'Is Nick very cross with me?' and a few tears trembled on her lashes and trickled down her cheeks.

'Hush, I will tell you all I know, but not if you are going to be upset,' Varuni told her firmly, wiping the tears away. 'Of course Nick is not cross with you. He is feeling all remorse for the fact that he did not save you from harm. He himself received injury from the falling timber, but his head is thicker than yours.' A chuckle escaped her lips. 'If you could have seen yourselves . . . both of you covered in fruit pulp!'

'Nick was hit too?'

'A glancing blow only.' Varuni gave a deep sigh. 'It was a sad day for Surin. The elephant did much damage to buildings and many people were injured, not only because of the animal but because of the panic in the crowd. The poor elephant was not to blame—they are not used to crowds and motor cars. Someone thoughtless and in too much haste to wait for proper clearance drove too close and scraped the animal's leg. He felt pain and became frightened and his boy could not control him. Two people were killed, Alex.' She squeezed her friend's hand tightly. 'You cannot imagine our alarm when we found you were not with us!'

'I somehow lost you all . . . and then I thought that Ben . . .'

'Ah, it was fortunate that Nick had already forbidden the boys to go near the elephants. He heard them planning to go, you see, and he knows that they can never be trusted.'

'W-where is Nick now?' Alex asked tentatively,

wondering what on earth she was going to say to him and feeling relieved when Varuni replied:

'It was necessary for him to return to Bangkok, but only when he was satisfied that you were out of danger. The others all went back the next day as planned.'

'And Ben?'

Varuni smiled. 'The young Ben did not wish to leave his sister, but Nick had a long talk with him and he was at last persuaded to return with Melanie and Warren, where he is now staying . . . you need have no concern for Ben.' It was a gentle order.

Alex gratefully accepted the drink which Varuni was offering, the water cool against her cracked, dry lips.

'What's the matter with me, Varuni? Apart from a cracked head, I mean.'

Varuni made the pillows more comfortable and smoothed down the sheet before answering.

'You have what every tourist gets eventually if they stay here long enough, a mild enteric germ.' She paused and looked at her consideringly. 'I think you had not been feeling too well, Alex, and did not say. If this ever happens again you must tell Nick and he will give you some tablets specially made for this complaint. You will find that all your friends are never without them in their medicine chest. And now, my dear Alex, you will not worry about anything. Somchai says that rest is the only cure for your poor head, and talking has wearied you. I will leave you for a while and you might sleep again. You will feel much better soon, I promise you.'

Alex let the soothing words drift over her and did as she was told, and Varuni was right in her advice. Each day Alex felt stronger until she was allowed to sit beneath the shade of a clump of palm trees on the edge of the orchard.

A family of ducks were making their way down to a small lake beyond where she was sitting, taking advantage of the slight breeze coming across the rice fields. Alex gave a satisfied sigh and thought how peaceful it all was, and knew she would be sorry to leave this tranquil and simple existence where everything seemed basic and straightforward.

She had no warning of his approach other than a footfall on the hard baked rutted earth as he came towards her, face grave, eyes hidden behind dark glasses.

'H-hello, Nick,' she managed coolly enough, while two spots of colour stained her cheeks and her heart raced erratically. 'How nice to see you.' She saw the discoloured flesh and ragged cut on his forehead and gave a gasp. 'Oh, heavens! Varuni told me you weren't badly hurt!'

'Hello, Alex . . . and she told you right. This looks worse than it is.' He dropped to the ground by her side. 'You're looking better than when I last saw you.' He gave a wry smile. 'You were looking like the wounded soldier home from the wars.'

Alex lifted a hand and tucked a strand of hair behind her ear. 'The bandage came off quite soon, once I stopped bleeding all over the place.' She plucked nervously at a leaf of maize growing near and began to shred it to pieces. 'I'm terribly sorry, Nick, I've been a dreadful nuisance to you.'

'Oh, a dreadful nuisance!' he came back, mocking her remorse. 'Ben's fine, by the way. Mel says to tell you he's no trouble and a definite good influence on her two. They all send their love.' Nicholas took off his glasses and thought for a moment. 'Why didn't you tell me you were feeling unwell, Alex?'

She gave a swift upward glance and found the

directness of his regard unnerving and looked down again, pulling a face.

'It was wrong of me, I know, but I didn't want to disrupt the weekend and be ...'

'... a nuisance.'

She had to smile at that. 'I didn't succeed very well, did I?' Her eyes were drawn once more to his forehead and her brow puckered. 'If I hadn't got lost you wouldn't have been hit ... I'm so sorry, Nick. D: does it hurt?'

Nicholas made a negative movement with his hand and said abruptly:

'Not as much as I deserve. A fine rescuer I turned out to be!'

'What nonsense! I won't have you talk that way,' she protested warmly. 'I was never so thankful to see anyone as I was when I saw you.'

'Hmm ... I'm beginning to wonder if there's something about you and danger that go together. Anyway, we're lucky, on all counts, that things have turned out as they have and no real harm done. Varuni tells me you feel fit enough to travel back. Do you feel up to doing part of the journey today?'

'Why, yes, I think so.'

'Good. We'll break our journey at Khorat, there's no rush and it will be better for you. Then we'll go on to Bangkok tomorrow. Somchai is collecting Varuni at Khorat, it's all arranged and they'll return in one go.'

'Is Rachan with you?'

'No, I'm alone.' He lifted a quizzical brow. 'Don't you trust my driving, Alex?'

'Yes, of course,' she said hurriedly, rising to her feet and taking his offered arm. The thought of a few hours alone with Nicholas was strangely exhilarating. 'I want to get back home to see Ben. He'll worry if I'm away too long,' she explained, covering her pleasure.

'Ah, yes, Ben,' reflected Nicholas thoughtfully.

Alex made her farewell to the farmer and his wife, expressing through Varuni her thanks for their hospitality. Somchai was waiting for Varuni at Khorat and they set off for Bangkok. There was time for Alex to have a short rest before the evening meal and then, dressed once more in her favourite sea-green silk jersey, she accompanied Nicholas to a secluded table for two on the roof-top dining room, which was surrounded by greenery and flowers. Alex found she was hungry, really hungry for the first time in days. The wine Nicholas ordered with the meal loosened her tongue and she was soon telling him about her work at the library and one or two funny incidents that had happened to her there. Nicholas was relaxed and attentive, drawing her out with his usual expertise.

The waiter brought coffee and liqueurs, offering Alex an orchid blossom with the compliments of the management. She thanked him prettily and fixed it to her dress, and Nicholas, after asking her permission to light a cigar, observed:

'Yes, you're looking like the Alexandra of old. You had me worried there at Surin . . . in fact, that blow on the head might in the long run have been fortuitous— I was feeling rather murderous at the time.'

Alex gave a low laugh and spoke feelingly. 'Don't I know it! And you had every right . . . but I remember I did manage to say I was sorry.'

His brows shot up and he replied sardonically: 'My dear girl, I couldn't stop you saying sorry! All our friends were looking at me with suspicious eyes, their imaginations running riot, I can assure you! What had this brute done to the poor, defenceless girl? I could hear them thinking! It was useless to protest my innocence.'

Alex burst out laughing. 'You're exaggerating.'

'Indeed I'm not! In the end Varuni suggested that I remove my presence as it was an upsetting influence.'

His words flustered her. Dear heavens, what had she said? Her voice was contrite: 'Oh, dear . . . what a nuisance I am to you, Nick.'

'No, I wouldn't say you were that,' he replied calmly. 'Tell me, have you always had this fear of being a burden, or is it something I personally bring out?'

'Why, I . . .'

'I suppose it must be attributed to having had a lonely childhood . . . it was lonely, wasn't it?' He smiled slightly at the flicker of surprise that crossed her face. 'Don't think that because Charles was a good friend and colleague that I'm not able to appreciate his limitations. And I can understand why eight years of self-imposed responsibility is hard to throw off. They've made nonsense of any hopes you may have had of being looked after yourself. I have a measure of sympathy for that suitor of yours back in England.'

'Why do you say "self-imposed"?' retorted Alex, and he lifted a placatory hand.

'Here we go again, those bristles are rising! Because, my dear girl, had you not been the kind of child to shoulder responsibility so thoroughly, your father would have been compelled to have done something about his children. While you were able to cope, and willing to cope with the succession of housekeepers and childminders, even sacrificing your own further education—because you needn't try and tell me that your teachers failed to advise you to go on to University, for I shan't believe you . . . then Charles, in his muddled, selfish way, was quite prepared to let

things remain as they were. Okay, so his realisation of
what he'd put upon you came a little late, but it
came—in the shape of his last will and testament, free-
ing you of the burden—that word again—of your
brother.'

'How do you know he just didn't think me capable?'
she asked with kindly scorn, and Nicholas shook his
head disbelievingly.

'Because you'd proved your capabilities over the
past eight years, you simpleton. You have this block-
age, Alex, that your father didn't love you . . . it sticks
out a mile. Well, he didn't show it as a father should,
but I guess he loved you as much as he was able.'

'You'd make a good P.R. man, Nick,' Alex informed
him dampingly, but his words had shaken her.

He gave a short laugh. 'I can even find it in my
heart to pity the man . . . he lost out on so much. You
must have given Charles hell every time he came
home. Looking more and more like your mother as
you grew older, reproach and contempt looking at him
out of those big blue eyes of yours . . . I guess it was
easier for him to stay away. Poor man, he was filled
with guilt and wasn't able to do a damn thing about it.
Buried himself deeper and deeper into the past and
when he found that his own future was doomed tried
to do recompense for your own.'

The curve of Alex's mouth was derisive. 'Quite the
philosopher, aren't you? And all this because I apolo-
gised for being a nuisance!'

'You had me fooled at first, with that cool, haughty
look of yours, but not any more. It's turned on as a
form of defence.' Nicholas drew on the cigar and
watched a thin spiral of smoke linger on the air before
turning clear, steady eyes upon her contemplatively.
'When you came round from that knock on the head

you were incoherent for a while, but it was apparent that you were concerned about what I would say. You became very agitated on that point. I joked earlier about it, but it seemed that you'd cast me to be the big bad ogre.' He paused. 'I shouldn't like to think, Alex, that you were really afraid of me.' The words were quietly spoken.

Alex stared at him, nonplussed, feeling her cheeks grow warm.

'I've never been frightened of you, Nick,' she managed at last, dropping her eyes to her hands in her lap, 'but only of the power you have over my life . . . and Ben's.'

He nodded thoughtfully. 'That's what I guessed. What I hoped. It's the future, yours and Ben's, that I would like to discuss with you, if you're not too tired?'

She looked up quickly at that, eyes questioning, but his face told her nothing. He took her silence as consent and continued almost clinically:

'I've been giving the whole situation some thought over the past few days, and I've come to the conclusion that the best solution would be for you to marry me,' and flicking a speck of cigar ash from his sleeve, Nicholas sat back and awaited her reaction.

CHAPTER SIX

ALEX stared at him incredulously, hardly able to believe her ears. She gave an uncertain laugh, saying:

'How absurd you are!' and then flatly: 'You must be joking.'

Nicholas raised his brows. 'Marriage may be many things, but I doubt either of us consider it to be a joke.' His lips twisted in a wry smile. 'Don't look so horrified, my dear. If the suggestion is abhorrent to you we'll forget it was ever voiced. But don't reject it out of hand. If you think about it calmly and rationally you'll find there's much to commend the idea.'

Calmly and rationally! If Alex had not been so amazed she would have burst into hysterical laughter—or tears. Was this a proposal of marriage? This cool assessing of facts? The setting was right ... the mystical, exotic East, an attractive, extremely eligible man, flowers and music. What right had calmness and rationality to intrude into such a perfect picture?

She searched his face again for some clue to his feelings. It was grave, eyes serious though not expressive. He was giving her no help.

'You've just thought of the idea ... right out of the blue,' she suggested, but even as the words sprang to her lips she knew them to be untrue, against character, and Nicholas shook his head.

'No. It's the obvious solution to the problem of Ben's future, but not necessarily the best. I personally can think of any number of suggestions that would,

I'm sure, give Ben a secure future, but inevitably I then come up against your own, and the boy's, views. I've been aware all along of your feelings in the matter. As for Ben . . .' He hesitated. 'Ben's reaction to you being lost at the Show, and your unfortunate accident, shook me, I will admit . . . and his behaviour precipitated the need to come to a decision. I asked Varuni to say nothing to you while you were recovering at Surin, but now you're stronger . . .'

'What happened?' she asked sharply. 'Is Ben all right? What are you keeping back?'

'Ben is perfectly well and happy,' Nicholas said firmly. 'He merely showed, in no uncertain manner, that you were the most important person in his life.' He paused. 'Everyone, of course, was upset about Surin, and when it was apparent that you were in no danger the Carrs, Suzanne and Ben returned to the hotel at Khorat while the rest of us went with you to the farmhouse. At the hotel Suzanne said something to upset Ben, I don't know what it was, anyway it culminated in him running away.' At her quick intake of breath he carried on smoothly: 'He was trying to make for Surin. Luckily he didn't get far and came to no harm, Warren was excellent with him, and the next day I had a good long talk with him and was able to persuade him to return to Bangkok with Mel and Warren, where he is now.'

The waiter arrived at this point to clear the coffee things and leave a bowl of fruit, and there was silence between them while he did so.

Alex's thoughts were a whirl of confused questions and conjecture, her eyes set on Nicholas across the white table cloth, taking in the calm profile, the relaxed line of his body. He looked as though he had just suggested an outing to the zoo and irrationally a rush of anger swept over her and, goaded, she remarked coolly:

'You surely don't ask me to believe that you're in love with me—or I with you?'

He sighed and leaned forward to crush the cigar. 'That, my dear Alex, would be insulting your intelligence, and I have no wish to cloud the issue with talk of love.' He paused to observe the effect of these words and continued repressively: 'When my wife and child were killed I was determined never again to tie myself down with the burden of such an emotion and I threw myself into work. It's easier for a man to make such a decision, especially if he's doing the work he loves. It was, perhaps, rather a drastic decision for a comparatively young man to take—I was twenty-six then—but it didn't seem so at the time, nor have I had occasion to regret it during the ensuing years.' He sat back and regarded her steadily. 'When I accepted the guardianship of Ben I assumed, in my ignorance, that life could continue as it had done in the past—why should one small boy upset it? As events have proved, I was wrong, but then I hadn't met Alexandra Jane, had I? I hadn't come up against her stubborn determination or her fierce protective instincts. In the weeks that I've known you, Alex, I've been at varying times infuriated and exasperated almost beyond the point of self-control . . .'

'I really can't see why you want to marry me, then!'

'I've explained why: Ben. And perhaps, poor fool, I feel that if someone doesn't take you in hand you'll kill yourself. Your propensity for attracting danger is positively terrifying.'

'That's unfair, Nick!'

'Maybe it is.' There was a gleam of amusement in his eyes for a second. 'However, despite your headstrong ways, Alex, you've commanded my respect and admiration for your loyalty to Ben, even if, at times, I thought it misplaced. You've a warm and friendly personality, are intelligent and have a sense of humour, and even when you're frowning, as now, you're extremely pleasing to the eye. All attributes highly commendable in a wife, wouldn't you say?' He reached out and plucked a grape from the cluster of fruit in the bowl. 'Aren't companionship, admiration and respect solid enough foundations on which to build a marriage?' he asked, and waited patiently for her answer.

'Yes.' She found it impossible to look at him. 'Yes, of course they are.'

'It would be a solution to a difficult problem. I need a wife, Ben needs a mother. You refuse to leave Ben and I am determined to fulfil the terms of Charles's will. Isn't it sensible for us to join forces and achieve a working arrangement?' His voice was mild and matter-of-fact.

Sensible! Oh, yes . . . it was sensible.

'Of course, you may think you're losing out on the bargain,' he continued musingly, when she didn't speak. 'I doubt I shall be easy to live with. Ben and I have more to gain. If it's totally impossible, please say, I won't be offended,' and the promise was dry.

'Yes! No . . . I don't know!' Alex pressed her fingers to her head despairingly. 'It seems an extraordinary idea!'

'There's no hurry. You may like the idea the more you think on it. It is, after all, a new one for you, while I have the advantage of living with it for a few days.'

'People don't marry for convenience in this day and age . . .'

'Probably more often than you think.' He shrugged

a shoulder. 'With age comes a certain amount of cyni-
cism, I'm afraid, and it seems perfectly natural and
sensible to weigh everything in the balance rather than
be swayed by the grand passion into doing something
illogical.'

Sense against sensibility, thought Alex bleakly.

'What about Suzanne?' she asked bluntly, and he
was clever enough not to dispute the question, merely
waited for her to go on. 'Everyone thinks that you and
Suzanne . . .'

'Everyone,' he repeated heavily, 'would do well to
mind their own business. You need not concern yourself with Suzanne.'

Indignation began to smoulder. 'That's all very
well,' she responded blightingly, 'and I'll be quite
willing to oblige if she'll do the same!' and not bother-
ing to conceal her mortification, she finished: 'She
knows *all* about Singapore!'

There was a pause and then Nicholas said mildly:
'I doubt that . . . unless you've told her.'

This stopped Alex in her tracks. 'I certainly
haven't!' and suddenly sure that Nicholas hadn't
either, she added lamely: 'How did she know?'

'From a man called Shipman. Do you remember I
used another bathroom that night? Well, it was Shipman's. He's a reporter and was in the foyer of the
hotel when we came in. He saw you, of course, and I
gave him the barest outline of what had happened and
he was quite happy for me to clean up in his suite.
Unfortunately he was covering the Loy Krathong Festival and recognised you. He thought I'd been string-
ing him along after that, naturally enough, I suppose,
and that I'd only pretended not to know who you were
to save embarrassment all round. I thought I'd convinced him a second time, but the trouble with Ship-

man is that he drinks too much and likes to tell a good story. I believe he took a shine to Suzanne once and didn't get anywhere. He would have enjoyed telling her about Singapore.'

'And has the story got around? Is this why you're offering to make an honest woman of me?'

He raised his brows quizzically. 'If it will make you see my proposal in a kindly light, then I'll say yes.'

'It won't. People can think what they like,' she responded shortly.

'In that case I'll tell you that so far as I'm aware the lurid story of Singapore is not common knowledge.'

Alex looked at him suspiciously, detecting amusement behind the words, but she could see no signs on the bland face opposite. So she needn't concern herself with Suzanne! She wondered what Suzanne would say about that. She rose when Nicholas suggested they walk through the flower garden, lit with lanterns, glad to stretch her legs. The blossoms were heady with perfume and their vivid colouring almost too bright to be believable. Stopping by a rail surrounding a fishpond, Nicholas said quietly:

'The main issue is whether you think Ben worth sacrificing the chance of finding "the grand passion".' His voice lingered sardonically on the words. 'In a few years' time his need for you will be gone.'

Alex stared down into the water, watching the pale shapes of the fish swimming in the depths. 'The same could be applied to yourself.'

She had to wait for his reply.

'I've already explained that I've had my taste of grand passion and see no necessity to repeat it.' Nicholas leaned against the rail and folded his arms across his chest. 'Folk will talk, of course, that's to be expected. I shall pretend to have fallen madly in love

with you . . . and you couldn't resist my fatal charms—
or perhaps that would be asking too much?' and his
eyes slanted down at her.

'I haven't said I'll do it yet,' she parried coolly, 'but
I can manage a lot for Ben's sake.'

'Yes, that's what I thought. Could you manage
enough, I wonder?'

'What do you mean?'

'I mean that although this marriage would theoreti-
cally be one of convenience in practice it would be a
true one in every sense of the word, with you sharing
my bed as well as my name.'

Alex's face flamed. 'Of course I realise that—I'm
not a fool.'

'I didn't think you were . . . just an innocent.' He
straightened. 'It's getting late and we have the journey
before us tomorrow.' He took her arm and led her
back through the dining room. As they approached
her room he said: 'Don't lose any sleep over this, Alex.
Think about it and let me know some time.'

Alex fumbled with the key and he took it from her,
opening the door and standing aside for her to enter.
The maid had been in and folded back the covers from
the bed and a small side light burned, making the
room welcoming. Nicholas followed her in and frowning slightly remarked brusquely:

'I'm not sure that I ought to have brought the
matter up tonight—but it seemed too good an opportunity to miss. Forgive me if I've tired or worried
you. You're beginning to look ethereal again.'

He was right as usual. A sense of weariness had
swept over her. There was also this ridiculous feeling of
wanting to burst into tears . . . and that would never
do. Cool practicality was the order of the day.

She turned to face him, and although it was an

effort to sustain the scrutiny of that clear, grey-eyed regard, replied in a reasonably steady voice:

'Yes, Nick, I will marry you.'

A tightening movement of his jaw was the only reaction to her words during the pause that followed. If she had realised how young and vulnerable she looked, standing there in the pool of light thrown by the lamp, she would have known the reason for the shortness of his tone when he did speak.

'I think you should sleep on it.'

'I won't change my mind.'

Nicholas twisted his mouth into some semblance of a smile that didn't quite reach his eyes. 'No. I know to my cost what a determined young woman you are. I also know you're headstrong and impulsive. I'll not have the accusation that you were not given enough time thrown at my head.'

Alex made an instinctive movement away, touching slender fingers to her forehead, eyes closed, the honey-gold lashes lying fanned across the smooth curve of her cheeks.

'I deserved that, I suspect.' She gave a small laugh. 'Poor Nick! You took on more than you bargained when you became my father's friend, didn't you? But then no one forced you to take us on, Ben and I. Just as no one is forcing me to accept your proposal.' Her hand dropped gracefully to her side and she turned slowly back, blue eyes pensive. 'What was it you said about the Thai people?' Her forehead creased. 'Something about each man being responsible for his own destiny? It's an interesting theory, don't you think? Perhaps you should have left me to my fate that night in Singapore . . .'

'And now you're being fanciful,' Nicholas broke in swiftly, and Alex pulled a rueful face and said lightly:

'Yes, I'm sorry. You deal in facts, not fancies, don't you? I won't change my mind, Nick, but if it makes you feel any better you can ask me again tomorrow.' She held out her hand, wanting to end the conversation. 'Shall we seal our bargain?'

His hand came up slowly and for a moment the clasp was easy, and then she found herself drawn irrevocably towards him and his lips touched hers, briefly, making no demands. Even so she couldn't help stiffening momentarily at the contact, stepping back quickly as she was released.

If he was aware of her reaction Nicholas didn't show it. Very much in control of the situation he observed calmly:

'Two seals—a businesslike one and a more fanciful one. Goodnight, Alex. Sleep well,' and on her murmured response he left the room, closing the door softly behind him.

Alex stood for a long moment when he had left her, the imprint of his lips still with her.

Each man is responsible for his own destiny. The words haunted her. What, she wondered bleakly, was hers to be?

As she threw clothes into her suitcase the next morning, paying little regard to their welfare, the doubts began to set in. How on earth had she got herself into such a crazy situation—what madness had possessed her to say 'yes' to Nicholas?

This last despairing question pulled her up short and she stopped in the act of forcing down the lid and told herself she knew exactly why she had said yes ... so who was kidding whom? Giving the lid a defiant thump she clicked the catch shut and the panic deepened and tightened into a hard knot in the pit of her stomach. Yes, she knew why, but she hoped desperately that Nicholas didn't.

She frowned and sat down limply on the side of the bed, searching through his words and the matter-of-fact logic that had prompted them. No, there was no indication to suspect that he had guessed—for one very good reason. Had he done so he would never have asked her to marry him.

Alex raised her head and challenged the accusing image in the dressing-table mirror opposite, and the blue eyes looked back at her pityingly. Love is not a word on this particular contract, Miss Templar. Can you cope with loving a man, knowing he doesn't love you?

She closed her eyes, blocking out her conscience. She hadn't wanted to love him she'd been fighting it for weeks, but it had made no difference in the end . . . and here she was, in a crazy situation where head and heart were in conflict—and it was driving her mad!

Unable to sit still, she began to pace the room, knowing that Nicholas would be coming for her soon and that she had to make up her mind what to do before then. If only she could have gone on hating him, how much easier it would be. She would just have said 'no' and that would have been that. Could she pretend indifference? If ever he guessed that she loved him she'd die of mortification!

She was back at the mirror again, and paying special attention to the spot where she had received the blow that knocked her out, she began to carefully brush her hair.

Well, he won't guess, will he, if you play your part well? You've shown in no uncertain manner your dislike of him, right from the start. The brush slowed and she allowed herself a wry smile. No, not right from the start . . . hadn't she fallen a little in love with him that night in Singapore? Yes, of course she had, in the silly, romantic fanciful way someone would who'd been rescued from a watery grave by an intriguing stranger. But all that nonsense had to be forgotten when the hateful Professor turned up ... and then it was easy to hate him.

But for how long, she questioned herself ironically, when each day getting to know him hating became harder and harder?

Alex remembered again those words he had used and what they offered. Companionship, admiration and respect. Could those feelings, in time, change to love? she wondered.

Now stop that! she told herself sharply, glaring at the mirror and throwing down the brush. Such thoughts mean certain heartache. You've got to accept what he can give you and not kid yourself there'll be anything more. As she prowled round the room again, a knock froze her into stillness.

The door needed to be opened. It would be Nicholas. Could she go through with it? She took a deep breath and grasped the handle.

'Good morning, Alex.' The grey eyes regarded her. 'Are you ready to go down?' Nicholas, tall and broad, solid and dependable, filled the doorway. Alex had a swift vision of him, tanned and freshly showered, strong neck rising from opened shirt, hair darkened by being damp, sleeves rolled back exposing sinewy forearms as his large capable hands took her case.

She made some reply. His voice, with its slight American intonation, soothed and delighted her. His touch beneath her elbow made her tremble and reduced her resolve to a crumbling rubble. How silly she was, she told herself blithely, her steps quick as she countered his long strides, her whole body alive and singing ... how silly! Of course she would go through with it!

They arrived in Bangkok just as the heat of the day was losing its intensity. The maid told them that Melanie and Warren had not yet returned but that the young masters were in the garden. Ben was playing in the pool with his two friends and seeing Alex walk down the path he heaved himself out of the water and rushed up to her, throwing his wet body forcibly at her. For a few moments Alex couldn't speak, so intense were her feelings at seeing him again. She remembered and relived those agonising minutes when she had thought him to be in danger at Surin and hugged him close. Glancing up, she found Nicholas's eyes upon them, and for some inexplicable reason felt herself flushing before the slightly cynical gleam in their expression. She lifted her chin defiantly. He was marrying her knowing that Ben was the motive. Why should he be surprised at their display of affection? They stayed for a time watching the boys' prowess on the diving board, but when the maid informed them that she had made tea, thirst drew them indoors.

'Are you going to tell them today? Mel and Warren, I mean?' Alex asked as she poured out, and Nicholas, turning from the window to receive his cup, replied: 'Yes, if you haven't changed your mind,' and he joined her on the sofa, the cushions sagging beneath his weight.

'I haven't changed my mind.'

'No, I didn't think you had—in fact, at a guess I should say that seeing Ben again has merely strengthened your resolve ... but I want you to be certain beyond any doubt before we spread the glad tidings.' His tone was almost disinterested.

'I'm quite certain.'

After a thoughtful nod Nicholas went on dryly: 'In that case you'd better brace yourself for the first hurdle. Mel will be delighted, she's a matchmaker at heart and will convince herself that it was all her idea before we know where we are. I'll go to the British Embassy tomorrow and find out the score—there's no reason why we should wait, is there?' and when Alex shook her head, he continued musingly: 'I know a chappie there who'll help get things moving, he owes me a good turn.'

'H-how long before . . .'

'. . . the ceremony can be performed? I have no idea, but at a guess I would think about ten days. Is there anyone you'd like brought over from England to be with you, Alex?' She must have shown surprise, for he added brusquely: 'You should have someone to give you moral support!'

'I've no near relative who means anything to me . . . except Ben, of course.'

'Of course.' The response came smoothly. 'Friends, then?'

Alex thought for a moment. 'I have a friend from school-days, but she's training to be a nurse and wouldn't be able to get leave at such short notice. If Mel and Varuni are with me I'll have enough support.' She smiled shyly. 'I've grown very fond of them both.' She hesitated. 'And you, Nick? Will you need moral support?'

He gave a thin smile. 'As my inclination is for as little fuss as possible I shall tell my family after the event. I won't subject you to my mother too soon—she has a nose like a ferret for a good story and she'd sniff ours out of you within a couple of days!'

Alex quite understood his reluctance. No mother

who loved her only son would countenance his marriage for the convenience of two strangers. She had seen a photograph of the Devlins; father, mother and three children, taken some years ago, and had envied their look of close-knit family happiness. Nicholas had told her that his father had returned to the ancestral acres in Ireland when his grandfather died and now had a stud of bloodstock horses that in equestrian circles made the name of Devlin world-famous. His two younger sisters were both married, with families, one living in America, the other in Australia. His mother—according to Mel still a beauty even though she was in her middle fifties—spent her time between the three countries and writing detective stories, so popular with devotees of that genre as to cause embarrassment when she was recognised.

Yes, on reflection, she quite understood why Nicholas didn't want a fuss, but she mildly resented the idea that he should suppose she felt the same. She placed her empty cup on the tray and with a hint of disappointment in her voice said:

'I've always longed for a white wedding, with a flowing veil and bridesmaids and perhaps a pageboy or two . . .'

Face shuttering his feelings, Nicholas replied with admirable self-control:

'I shall, of course, fall in with whatever you wish,' and then, when Alex could contain herself no longer and leaned back, helpless with laughter, he said quietly: 'Why, you little madam! You said that to give me a few bad moments!' and his hand streaked out and grasped her wrist, drawing her to him.

Still bubbling with mirth, Alex spluttered: 'Oh, Nick! If you could have seen your face! It was a picture!'

'Very likely,' he came back, the grimness of his tone belied by the gleam in his eye, 'and now I'll . . .'

She was not to hear what Nicholas intended, for at that precise moment Melanie and Warren burst into the room with delighted greetings. Afterwards Alex was to wonder whether things would have been different had their friends delayed their return by even a few minutes. As it was Nicholas released her wrist and leisurely rose to his feet, turning as Melanie cried:

'Sorry we're so late . . . the traffic was dreadful. Alex, my dear, how are you? Let's have a look at you,' and coming round the sofa, she searched Alex's face as she clasped her hands warmly between her own. 'Still a bit peaky, but looking better than when we saw you last . . . Oh, dear, all that blood! And Nick . . . goodness, that forehead of yours is turning an interesting colour, makes you look most rakish. Well? Do you think she'll do?'

Nicholas smiled faintly and looked down at Alex, eyes hooded. 'Oh, yes, Mel, I think she'll do.'

'Glad to have you back, Alex,' and Warren came forward and patted her shoulder kindly. 'You did rather worry us, you know, but no harm done, eh?'

Nicholas took her hand and drew her to her feet, placing his other arm round her shoulders. 'On the contrary,' he said candidly, 'rather the reverse. We'd like you both to be the first to know our news. Alex and I are going to be married.'

Stunned silence followed this proclamation and then Warren, recovering quicker than his wife, said with obvious pleasure:

'My dear fellow, congratulations . . . and Alex, I'm delighted, and wish you every happiness.'

'Good heavens!' breathed Melanie at last, her eyes going from Alex's rosy red face to Nicholas's amused

one. 'How absolutely marvellous . . . oh, Alex!' and
she hugged the English girl hard. Then she gave Nicholas a hearty kiss, exclaiming: 'As for you—you've
shown some sense at last, you clever man!'

'Yes, I have, haven't I?' Nicholas agreed, his amusement growing, glancing knowingly down at Alex, who
refused to meet his eyes.

Melanie gave the younger couple a shrewd look.
'Well, there's nothing like a spot of drama to help
things along,' and slanting her husband a triumphant
grin, she chortled: 'And didn't I tell you it would
happen, Warren? Yet I still can hardly believe it!
Good gracious, this deserves a drink . . .' and by the
time the glasses and champagne had been procured
and a short but sincere toast been given by Warren,
Alex realised that the first hurdle was over and had not
proved to be so difficult as she had first imagined.

Later, when she and Melanie were together, Alex
said:

'I hope you don't mind having me here as well as
Ben, Mel. Nick rather takes things for granted sometimes. I mean, I could easily go to a hotel, or even
back to the apartment . . .'

'Oh, no, you couldn't. Nick's quite right about that,
even though it's a bit like shutting the stable door
when the horse has bolted.'

'What do you mean?'

Melanie shook her head in wonder. 'I mean it's a bit
late in the day for propriety. There are those who
think you've been sharing his bed as well as his apartment for a long time, honey.' She took in the blush
that swept over her young friend's face with kindly
amusement, assuring her firmly: 'It'll be much nicer
for you to be married from here, and it won't be for
long, will it? Nick's not allowing you to keep him wait-

ing, is he?' and her eyes twinkled roguishly.

'Oh, well, if you're sure . . .' responded Alex feebly, and Melanie said bluntly:

'Quite sure . . . and Warren's tickled pink that you asked him to give you away. Where's Nick taking you for your honeymoon?'

'That, my dear Mel, is the next thing on the agenda,' came Nicholas's smooth voice from the doorway, and he crossed to Mel's chair and persuaded her out of it. 'Why don't you hurry along that delicious meal you've invited us to share and leave us alone?' he urged her teasingly.

'Oh, very well. I know when I'm not wanted,' replied Melanie indulgently. She shook her head at them reproachfully. 'What a sly pair you are . . . it sure takes some getting used to. Alex honey, don't let this man bully you into having all his own way, will you?' She chuckled and made for the door. 'But then I don't think I need worry . . . oh, oh, how the mighty are fallen!' and still laughing, she left them.

'The mighty being me,' observed Nicholas wryly, and let his eyes rest on Alex pensively. 'You appeared startled at the idea of a honeymoon . . . we shall have to take one, it will be expected of us.'

'Yes. Yes, of course. I just hadn't thought, that's all.'

Nicholas eased himself down, settling himself in the corner of the sofa so that he could see her without straining, and crossed his long legs, body relaxed. Alex resented this ability of his to be so sure of himself, knowing it to be unfair, for that was part of his charm . . . and yet she had a perverse wish to see him ruffled, just once.

'Where would you like to go?' Nicholas was undeterred by her silence.

'I don't mind.' Goldie, the Carrs' labrador bitch, pushed open the door and waddled into the room, greeting Alex profusely, her tail thumping, and grateful for something to do Alex leaned forward to stroke her.

'I suppose what I really mean is, what sort of a place would you like to go to, in the few days I'll be able to wangle off?' Nicholas went on, stretching his hands to the back of his head and pondering on the situation. 'I shall have to take work with me, I'm afraid, my publisher's deadline is looming up. So where? And don't,' he continued with dangerous silkiness, 'say that you don't mind, or I'll give you the shaking you deserved earlier, broken head or no!'

Alex was obliged to smile at that and watched Goldie change her alliance, settling herself heavily against Nicholas's legs.

'I don't know the country well enough to say, do I? and I truly ... er ... wherever you decide will do, honestly.'

'Mm ... four days isn't enough to do much with.' Nicholas frowned, thinking hard as he pulled affectionately at Goldie's ear, finally commenting: 'Kasem has a house just beyond Pattaya. It's on the coast, quite private, yet within easy reach of the bright lights if we want them. How does that sound?'

'Lovely.'

'Good. I'll have a word with Kasem, but I doubt there'll be any problem. There'll be plenty to occupy ourselves with—Kasem has a boat and there's some interesting islands off the shore and when I have to work you can swim or sunbathe.'

'Perhaps I could help you. Type or read-over?' suggested Alex diffidently, and Nicholas gave a short laugh.

'My dear girl, I shan't make you work on your

honeymoon.'

'Well, it won't be a proper one, will it?' she pointed out reasonably, 'and you'll be working.'

'Of course it will be a proper one, Alex, why should you suppose otherwise?' His tone was mildly challenging. 'By the way, I've told Ben about us.'

This brought her head round. 'You have? What did he say?' When he didn't answer at once she repeated her question a little more sharply. 'Nicholas! What did he say? Was he pleased?' She found herself on her feet. Why wasn't he speaking? Was Ben going to object? and her heart began to thump madly.

Nicholas pursed his lips and replied tranquilly:

'He seemed pleased enough ... gave me his undivided attention for at least two minutes before rushing off to engage in a war game with the boys. Children are funny creatures. When you least expect it they create havoc and when you think you've dropped a bombshell they hardly react.'

'But what did he say?' Alex persisted, and Nicholas rose without haste to his feet, humping Goldie with kindly force out of the way.

'I believe his exact words were "Great! Now you won't be sending Alex away." Getting to the hub of the matter as children often do.' There was a hard core to the bantering tone. 'It's important that he doesn't suspect the real reason. You won't forget to help the illusion along, will you?'

She couldn't meet the ironic gleam in his eyes and looked down, murmuring: 'No, I won't forget.'

'Good. Then shall we start practising?' Nicholas suggested blandly, taking her in his arms.

This time the kiss was more demanding. For a few moments they stood close and then voices and feet were heard the other side of the door and they broke apart. As everyone began to pour into the room, making for the dining table, Alex moved stiffly away, colour heightened, and unable to meet Nicholas's thoughtful gaze.

CHAPTER SEVEN

THE advantage of having friends in official places meant that their plans went ahead without unnecessary delay.

Varuni, when told, was overjoyed on hearing of the forthcoming wedding, dark eyes glowing as she conveyed in her gentle, dignified way her happiness for them both. Her brother too added his congratulations and seemed delighted to be able to lend them his house at Pattaya.

Varuni also displayed her eagerness to help in the matter of a wedding dress, and it was with this in mind that she invited Alex to her home, a Thai house set in the centre of a walled garden, like a small oasis, in a busy part of Bangkok. Alex had noticed that the city was a hotch-potch of planning, and certainly no one would ever have guessed that behind the wall was a shaded garden, lush and green and cool.

Varuni greeted her with her usual mixture of warmth and shyness, first making a low *wai*, and then kissing Alex Western fashion on the cheek.

Alex knew that Varuni had been sent to England as a child of eleven to secure a good education and a knowledge of the language ... the Khomangs were great anglophiles. She had then gone from the small boarding school to art school, having shown a flair for design. On her arrival back in her own country she had, with her father's help, set up in business on her own.

'Many of our people are poor and their chances of employment are limited,' Varuni confessed, slipping off her shoes, as was the Thai custom, and leaving them outside the door before entering the house. Alex copied her and padded barefoot over the highly polished teak floor. 'It is right that I should pass on my knowledge in this manner . . . and they are good girls.'

Alex had been shown round the workroom, a sea of faces behind sewing machines, finding the atmosphere rather like a sewing class at a girls' school, especially the giggling, and they all looked very young. Alex was taken through, feeling like Royalty, inspecting the garments, and then Varuni took her into the main part of the house.

'I think I have the very material you are looking for,' Varuni now announced as she invited Alex to sit on one of the cushions scattered on the floor. She sank down herself, her legs tucked gracefully to one side, and began to pour tea set on a low table nearby. 'But you must say if you do not think it will suit,' she continued, her smile serene. 'You will not have seen anything so far here that would be acceptable—we Thais have a love of colour that would not do for what you want. But I have something on one side for you to consider,' and Varuni took a small hand bell and rang it and a few seconds later one of the girls brought in a bolt of silk, handing it to her mistress. With a smile the girl was dismissed and Varuni opened it out and offered it to her friend.

Alex took the cream silk between her fingers and gave a sigh of pleasure, saying simply:

'It's beautiful, Varuni, and exactly what I'm looking for. How clever of you.'

Varuni gave her gentle smile and smoothed her hand across the material in satisfaction. 'I am happy you are pleased. We shall now discuss the style and between us we shall design the perfect dress.' Her eyes appraised the English girl for some time, head tilted consideringly and presently she went on: 'I think it will be simple ... neither you nor the silk have any need for distraction. And so, my dear friend, we will make you beautiful for Nicholas, I promise.'

Alex was reminded of Varuni's promise on the eve of her wedding day. It had been a day of surprises, the biggest being the arrival at midday of Nicholas's cousin and his wife, Edward and Eleanor Mansel, from England. They had all met up at a reception at the American Embassy and had just that moment dropped the couple off at their hotel, and it was Eleanor's 'See you in church tomorrow,' that had brought the wedding dress to mind. Perfect in every detail, the dress was ready and waiting, and as lovely as Alex had dreamed or hoped it to be.

'Do you mind if we call in at the apartment before I take you on to Mel and Warren's? There's something I want to pick up.' Nicholas, driving the Pontiac, broke into her thoughts and demanded her attention.

Alex stirred in her seat. She felt tired, but more in spirit than in body. 'No, I don't mind,' she answered. 'It's not late, is it?'

Nicholas lifted a hand from the steering wheel and turned his wrist, glancing briefly at the luminous dial of his watch.

'Just after twelve. Not late, considering a normal Embassy do,' he observed.

Just after twelve. So it was already today.

'I thought the evening went well. Did you enjoy yourself?' Nicholas asked presently, his voice non-committal, almost as if he were thinking of something else and merely making conversation.

'Oh, yes, thank you.' How stilted that sounded! Alex

went on hurriedly: 'You didn't tell me that Eleanor and Edward were coming over f-for the wedding.'

'There was no point until I knew they'd make it for certain,' Nicholas pointed out with his usual good sense. 'I knew they were due to arrive in the country around this time anyway and I cabled on the offchance that they might be able to come a little earlier than planned.'

'Was Edward surprised when you told him why?'

'No. That's not Edward's style.'

Alex became silent. I'll bet it's not, she thought. Edward Mansel had the same self-assured air as Nicholas, neither giving anything away. 'Is he over here on holiday?' she probed.

'Partly. Edward and my uncle run an air-freight company, but Edward also has a finger in the antique trade as well. He manages to combine the two interests. It's purely a holiday for Eleanor.'

'How long have they been married?'

Nicholas frowned, finding it necessary to work that question out. 'About a couple of years.' He paused and said reflectively: 'At the time Edward surprised everyone. He seemed a confirmed bachelor.'

Just as you must have seemed a confirmed widower, Alex thought bleakly, but with one subtle difference— Edward is deeply in love with his wife.

'Are you close? Cousins sometimes can be.' It was easier chatting than thinking.

'Yes. I suppose he's the nearest I have to a brother,' said Nicholas. 'We were always palmed off on to our grandparents in Ireland for school holidays. We must have been a sore trial to them, but they never let on.' He gave her a quick aside. 'I hope you'll like Edward.'

'I'm sure I shall,' Alex assured him, but in truth, she wondered. She found Edward Mansel slightly in-

timidating. She could see a family resemblance in the
dark hair and brows, maybe in the jawline, but
Edward's eyes were blue, not grey, and although he
had Nicholas's height he didn't have his breadth. Slim
and elegantly dressed, Edward was the possessor of a
pair of sleepy eyes, which Alex suspected missed nothing, and a languor reminiscent of a cat.

'You seemed to be getting along well with Eleanor,'
observed Nicholas, and this time Alex could reply
truthfully.

'I like her. She's easy to get on well with.'

Eleanor Mansel was twenty-three, a girl saved from
plainness by a pair of large, beautiful hazel eyes and a
warm, friendly manner. She had a teasing way with
her husband that led Alex to believe that perhaps
Edward was not so unapproachable after all, and she
deeply envied them their relationship.

Yes, in the short time she had known Eleanor, Alex
felt she had found an ally should she need one, and
there was no doubt that the presence of the English
girl had helped her during a difficult part of the evening.

It had been silly of her not to realise that Suzanne
would be at the Embassy reception that evening. Eleanor saw her first and whispered to Alex:

'My goodness, this girl's a striking beauty!'

Alex had turned to look in the direction of Eleanor's
gaze and became aware that Suzanne was making her
way towards their party. With her dark hair immacu-
ately groomed and make-up flawless, Suzanne looked
as though she had been poured into her scarlet evening
dress, which fitted where it touched. It was a dress that
needed nerve to wear and Suzanne carried it off
superbly. If she had set out with the intention of out-
shining her rival then she succeeded. Alex was wearing

what she herself had considered to be a rather sophis-
ticated dress the colour of wild clover, but next to the
scarlet of Suzanne's it became almost colourless and
drab.

Alex wasn't helped by the fact that Nicholas seemed
remote and at his most enigmatic, and so she was
grateful for Eleanor's support in the conversation,
for Suzanne's greeting to her was perfunctory. Her
eyes flicked Alex up and down with hardly concealed
challenge and then she pointedly ignored her.

After the dinner came the dancing, and Alex didn't
lack partners. At one time she saw Nicholas with
Suzanne. They were not talking and their steps
matched beautifully. It was a bitter pill when her own
dance with him was a total loss, full of tension and
awkwardness, and she felt relief when it was over.

Once, as Suzanne sailed past, vibrant and sparkling,
Alex turned to Eleanor and said wistfully:

'She's very attractive, isn't she?' and Eleanor had
nodded, adding guardedly:

'Perhaps a little too overpowering? Or does that
sound like sour grapes?' and they both had laughed at
that, with Alex saying ruefully:

'I feel totally eclipsed,' and hunching her shoulders
in pretty despair.

'No one ever eclipses the bride on her wedding day,
you can take that from me,' came the surprising reply,
and after giving her companion a startled look, Alex
murmured:

'I hope you're right.'

She contrived as naturally as possible to steer clear
of any chance of a private conversation with Suzanne.
The size of their party helped, but it was Warren,
standing up to offer Suzanne his seat next to Alex,
who innocently brought them together.

For a moment neither said anything and then the American girl offered Alex a cigarette, which was refused, coming straight to the point.

'You know, I underestimated you. God knows how you've managed it.' She drew on the cigarette, held between fingers tipped with scarlet, and contemplated Alex through the smoke. 'I still say you're not his type, Nick usually steers clear of the vestal virgin look. Of course, you have a hint of Martine about you . . . but I doubt you'll keep him long on that.' She arched her delicately drawn brows. 'I haven't decided on your motives yet. A father complex, I wonder, or a meal ticket? Or is it just conceivable that beneath that touch-me-not exterior of yours there beats a lovelorn heart?' She watched as a dull tide of heat rose slowly into Alex's face. 'My God, you poor mouse! I only hope you know what you're doing.' She smiled seductively. 'If you want any lessons on how to please him, let me know . . .'

'Excuse me, Alex, do you care to dance?'

Edward stood before her and Alex rose, zombie-like, and went without a word. Edward, who at the request of his wife to ask Alex for a dance had obeyed with the merest lift of his brows at the urgency of the appeal, set out to get to know this girl his cousin was marrying the following day. He thought her a little too coolly reserved for his taste and was surprised at Nick's choice, but was willing to concede he could be mistaken. Although he applied skilful use of his charm he was in for a disappointment. For the majority of the dance Alex was quiet and withdrawn, utterly passive and almost monosyllabic. Towards the end, however, she startled him by saying right out of the blue:

'Edward, did you know Nick's first wife?'

He eyed her warily. 'Martine? Yes, I knew her

slightly.'

'Was she American?'

'Yes.' The music stopped. 'Why do you ask, Alex?'

She shrugged and gave a quick smile which didn't quite reach her eyes. 'Oh, I wondered. Nick doesn't talk of her, you see.'

'I'm sure he would answer any questions you would care to ask,' Edward told her carefully, and blue eyes swept round in alarm.

'Oh, I'm sure he would ... I ... It doesn't matter ...' she finished, and led the way off the floor. Edward, following, found his eyes moving to the figure in scarlet, now dancing a flamboyant and highly entertaining tango with a Frenchman. He wondered uneasily what it was that Suzanne had said that had upset Nicholas's bride-to-be.

Alex, her head resting on the upholstery of the Pontiac's front seat, was wondering why they were on their way to the apartment. She moved fractionally to allow herself the pleasure of an unguarded appraisal of Nicholas in the kindly darkness of the car. Her eyes devoured his profile hungrily, noting with concern that it seemed more drawn than usual. She knew he had been pushing himself hard work-wise and if nothing else she might be able to persuade him to relax a little during the next few days.

Relax! She frowned dismally at the word. At the moment she felt as though she would never be able to relax again. For some time now her life existed as though in an obstacle race. Each meeting with Nicholas left her drained and she hoped with all her might that once they settled down into some semblance of routine, without the eyes of the world upon them, it would become easier for her. The biggest hurdle was tomorrow and she would have Warren's support, bless him ... Suddenly alert, she quickly counted the hours. Not tomorrow—today. In twelve hours she would be Mrs Nicholas Devlin.

'You're very quiet, Alex. Tired?' Nicholas pulled to a halt at an intersection and turned to her. 'Nervous about tomorrow?'

'Not unduly,' she returned, forcing herself to make conversation. 'I think Mel's more nervous than either of us!'

Nicholas gave a smile and drove on. 'I wonder if we've been wise, giving her carte-blanche with all the arrangements?'

'I've told her we don't want a fuss, but the poor dear can't comprehend. She has a three-tier wedding cake all planned.'

'Good God, she hasn't!' exclaimed Nicholas with a groan, swinging into the courtyard, the apartment building looming up out of the darkness. 'What the hell shall we need that for, with hardly a dozen guests to cater for?' The Pontiac slid smoothly into the parking space and he switched off the engine and lights. They were surrounded by darkness and silence.

'It seemed easier to give in on that point,' confessed Alex with a small laugh. 'She tells me that the top tier will be cut and eaten, the second saved for Christmas—it is, after all, only four weeks away—and the third ...' She stopped short, oddly at a loss.

'And the third?' Nicholas asked, his hand poised on the door handle.

Alex could have bitten her unruly tongue. Nothing would drag the word christening from between her lips.

'Why, it will be saved for Easter,' she finished lamely. 'Poor Mel feels cheated over such a small and informal reception ...'

'And is convinced it's all my doing,' remarked Nicholas dryly as he heaved himself from the car and walked round to open her door. 'I can quite see I'm to blame.'

'It's easier that way,' agreed Alex, negotiating her departure from the Pontiac unsteadily due to a long skirt and high heels. She accepted Nicholas's steadying hand and waited while he locked up, and as they walked towards the building, went on: 'I couldn't convince her I didn't want a fuss either, and as your back's broad, and deep down in Mel's eyes you can do no wrong, I left it that way.'

They gained the lift and as they began to ascend Nicholas said surprisingly:

'Maybe I allowed myself to be convinced too easily too.' He thrust hands in trouser pockets and leant against the wall, a rather brooding look on his face.

Alex stared. 'You didn't, but it's rather late to do anything about it now, isn't it?' She hesitated and then added curiously: 'What made you say that?'

'I was remembering Edward and Eleanor's wedding,' and on that rather cryptic note the doors opened and they emerged on the sixth floor, Nicholas delving into his pockets for the key.

'We let Mel persuade us into having a church ceremony, she'll have to be satisfied with that,' Alex stated flippantly, not quite understanding his mood, and following him into the apartment.

'Few people are satisfied with what they have,' Nicholas observed enigmatically, feeling for the table lamp. As the room sprung into subdued light he said over his shoulder: 'Would you like a drink?' and taking off his jacket he threw it over the back of a chair and made for the drinks table.

Alex leaned on the closed door and slipped off her

evening shoes, wriggling her toes in relief.

'No, thanks, but I'd love coffee.' She left him pouring out a drink for himself and made her way into the spotless kitchen. Plugging in the kettle, she wondered what she would find to do all day with such a competent maid as Malee part of the household. A momentary feeling of panic swept over her at the thought of the future, which she as quickly thrust down, busying herself setting the tray. She heard the telephone begin to ring and waited a few seconds for it to be answered, then padded out of the kitchen, finding the room empty.

She had just time to hear someone say: 'Nicky darling, is that you?' when Nicholas emerged from his room and wordlessly she handed the telephone over and walked stiff-backed into the kitchen.

Anger coursed through her veins. How dared that girl ring up! Wasn't she ever going to let go? Alex found herself clinging to the sink top, trembling violently. She would have to say something. She could go through this marriage, but not if she was unsure of Nicholas's intentions regarding Suzanne.

Nicholas was stretched out in one of the deep armchairs, head back, eyes closed, a half empty glass still held in one hand. She stood for a moment, breath held, before letting it go in one long-drawn-out sigh. Damn Suzanne . . . and damn him, too! The glass in his hand began to tilt and she reached out and began to take it from his inert fingers. As it was slowly withdrawn the fingers tightened and closed and she found his lashes raised and the grey eyes watching her.

'I thought you'd dropped off.' His regard was unnerving and Alex moved to the other chair where she busied herself with the coffee things.

Nicholas drawled: 'That wouldn't be very gallant of

me, would it?' He emptied the glass in one swallow and added dryly: 'And I'm not going to turn into an alcoholic, Alex, so don't look so disapproving.'

'I didn't know I was . . . and there's no need to be gallant with me.' Anger was a help sometimes. Play the gallant to Suzanne Miles, she told him silently.

Nicholas reached for the much worn dictionary from his desk and lazily thumbed its pages. Alex was becoming used to this love of words of his. Words were discussed and argued over constantly, and he had even drawn Ben into the habit now. It was becoming quite a competitive game between him and the Carr boys, encouraged by Nicholas.

Alex sneaked a look beneath her lashes while he was occupied. There was something niggling at him tonight, she decided uneasily, a cutting edge to his tongue now and again that was making him un-approachable. She cast her mind back and hoped she wasn't the culprit.

Nicholas had now found what he was looking for and it was causing him some amusement, although the twist to his mouth was downward. He closed the dic-tionary with a snap and dropped it back on to the desk.

'You're quite right to reject the word gallant,' he pronounced. 'Being "politely amorous" with one's intended wife is a little out-moded, don't you think?' He watched the slight flush creep over Alex's cheeks before rising and indolently making for the hi-fi equipment. He selected a record and put it on and when the music was coming through to his satisfaction he returned and reached down to pull her slowly to her feet.

'What did you think to the dancing this evening, Alex?'

She was quite bewildered. 'The dancing?' she echoed uncertainly, feeling the tension growing between them despite the casualness of the question.

'Yes. Did it inspire you?'

There should have been some clue to what he was getting at, but for the life of her she couldn't fathom what it was. She aimed for lightness.

'Well, I didn't do much. The Ambassador danced more on my feet than the floor, and Warren held me as if I would break. Edward was most proficient . . .' She took a breath and had inspiration. 'Oh! You mean Suzanne and the Frenchman! The tango!'

'No, I do not mean the tango,' he came back evenly. 'I mean the common-or-garden waltz. Shall I refresh your memory?' He took her in his arms but made no attempt to dance although the music was in waltz time and had presumably been put on for that purpose.

Alex fixed her eyes on the front of his evening shirt, her thoughts in wild turmoil. She swallowed hard before demanding:

'There's a reason behind all this, isn't there? I . . . can't believe it's anything to do with dancing.'

'You're right, dancing is only incidental.' His voice was clipped and he turned away, frowning, deep in thought, before swinging back and regarding her intently. Alex moistened her lips with the tip of her tongue. She had come up against Nicholas in many moods ranging from anger to kindly consideration, but tonight she couldn't place him. There was a sardonic twist to tone and expression that implied some inner emotion being firmly held in check. She wished she hadn't taken her shoes off . . . how could she retain any dignity standing in bare feet? And perhaps dignity was all she was left with . . .

Her chin came up. 'What's the matter, Nick?' Her voice was cool, but her pulse raced as he came slowly towards her.

'This,' was the laconic reply, and he placed his hands on the smooth golden-tan flesh of her shoulders, her skin burning at his touch. She stiffened involuntarily and Nicholas said flatly: 'You're frightened to death of me, aren't you?'

'No,' she managed between dry lips.

His hands continued along and down, taking the narrow straps of her dress with them. 'No?' he queried grimly, bending his head to touch the curve of neck and shoulder, his lips tantalising, his breath warm. 'No? You freeze like a scared rabbit whenever I touch you! If you're not frightened of me, why the hell do you flinch when there's physical contact between us?' He let her go and such was the grip that she staggered slightly. 'I've allowed for normal pre-wedding nerves, but this is something more.' He caught up the empty glass and swung away to refill it. Splashing out the liquid, he went on: 'Edward's coming has made me realise just what I'm asking you to take on . . . seeing him with Eleanor . . .' He tossed the drink down his throat almost angrily, then staring beneath lowered brows. 'I'm beginning to wonder if I've the right to deny you the chance of happiness like theirs . . . whether you know what you're letting yourself in for.'

'That's my decision—and of course I know . . . there's no need to wrap it up, Nick.'

'By personal experience—or romantic fiction?' The question came back hard and giving an angry exclamation he declared harshly: 'Don't try and kid me that you've been to bed with a man, because I won't believe you.'

'Should I apologise? Is it a crime?' demanded Alex

explosively. 'Would you rather I'd slept around?'

'It might be better for us both if you had.'

'Well, there's still time, I suppose,' she retorted with heavy sarcasm. 'The wedding's not for a few hours yet—I'll go and see if I can find someone to oblige!'

'Now you're being offensive,' came the biting reply.

'There's no pleasing you, Nick!' she cried out, furious with him and herself. 'How can I prove I'm going into this with my eyes open?' She flung away and paced for a few seconds and then rounded on him. 'Oh, I know what's happened! Your fine cousin's in the throes of the grand passion,' she rolled the words magnificently, mocking him, 'and your conscience is troubling you. Well, it's nice to know you have one, but I promise I'll not berate you in the future for taking advantage of my innocence! How's that?' She stood glaring at him, breasts rising and falling in agitation, suddenly frowning as a thought struck her. 'Or maybe it's not just conscience—maybe it's jealousy? Has Edward shown you what you'll be missing? Are *you* having second thoughts yourself, Nick? You say you're thinking of me, but perhaps it's more a way of saying *you* want to back out,' and she threw the words out challengingly.

'I'm giving you the chance to change your mind. Back there, in the lift, you said it was too late to do anything—well, it's not! I want you to get that into your stubborn head! It's not too late!'

'I have no intention of changing my mind.' Her eyes swept to the telephone and back. 'But perhaps there's someone who has changed yours for you? Nicky darling!' The endearment was an excellent imitation.

'Someone has.' His voice was dulcet.

Her heart contracted and plumeted sickeningly.

'Ben has,' he went on smoothly. 'If we make a mess of this marriage of ours he'll suffer too, and he deserves better than that.'

'If, if! I didn't think the great Professor Devlin ever made a mess of anything! Oh, come on, that's a bit weak—and so are the eleventh-hour scruples!' She raised her brows, adding scornfully: 'I wonder if it's your vanity that's at stake?'

'Just what do you mean by that?'

'Well, all this being worried by my reactions ... it's rather a blow to your fatal charms, isn't it? You're much more used to being able to, pick and choose, aren't you? Well, the fault may lie with me ... I mean, I must be odd not to succumb to the Devlin touch, don't you think?'

'Do go on. This is interesting.'

She was obliged to. She'd gone too far to let his icy politeness daunt her. 'Maybe you should find out whether I'm frigid before lumbering yourself with a wife who can't bear your touch! Although it works both ways, doesn't it? How do I know you're not a lousy lover?' She lifted a disdainful shoulder. 'Of course, I doubt that ... I mean, if Suzanne's satisfied then I suppose I should be.' She saw him stiffen and an arrested look come on to his formidably grim face. She arched her brows and her voice became sickly sweet. 'Oh, I'm sorry! Perhaps I shouldn't have mentioned Suzanne, but you know how it is when we girls get together ... little confidences drop out. *She* went into raptures ... but then,' and her voice hardened, 'I'm not Suzanne, am I? Still, as you say, there's time. We wouldn't want the great Devlin contract ruined because we didn't suit in bed, would we? Shouldn't we both find out—before it's too late? Nicky darling?'

Their eyes locked for a long moment. Nicholas's

face was curiously wiped of expression—Alex's was a mixture of anger and proud defiance. Then Nicholas turned and strode to the door. Alex watched him go, so full of conflicting emotions that when the realisation swept over her that he was walking out on her she was ready to sink to the floor with mortification! God, what had she done? she despaired inwardly.

His hand came up to knock down the catch, the lock sounding abnormally loud. Moving with quiet deliberation, Nicholas crossed to the record and switched it off, the music dying, and he came towards her, pulling off his tie with a slow and lazy gesture as he did so.

Alex stood frozen, all breath suspended, unable to speak or move, her eyes fixed on him while a turmoil of thoughts chased wildly round in her head. What a fool she was, to challenge a man like Nick! Now what to do? Make a joke of it? No, they were past the joking stage by the look on his face. Brazen it out, coolly and calmly? Impossible. She was neither cool nor calm. If only she could read his mind . . . he wouldn't take her at her word—would he? No, of course he wouldn't! He was playing with her, like a cat with a mouse. He was right up to her now and she could see no help in those clear grey eyes. Well, she wouldn't ask for any. She lowered her own, fixing them on the hollow of his throat rising out of the half-opened shirt. Now cuff-links were being studiously removed, without haste, and dropped into trouser pocket. Wretched, wretched man! Still no sign that he would let her off. Suddenly she knew that he wasn't going to—had no intention of doing so . . . unless she asked. The challenge was now his.

And then: 'I think you may be right, Alexandra. Yes, perhaps we should both find out.'

His voice was deeply contemplative and his hands

reached out to take the clips from her hair, allowing it to fall into a silken mass round her shoulders.

One word, Alex, one word and he'll stop, she told herself weakly, knowing even as his hands touched her that she would go through with it.

Ah, sweet heaven ... did he understand that she knew nothing?

CHAPTER EIGHT

'HEY! Alex, wake up, lazy-bones!'

Alex stirred, frowned and opened her eyes, blinking at the light, sleep still holding her.

Melanie shook her shoulder. 'My dear girl, are you going to sleep the whole of the day away? What about this wedding? You're not intending keeping poor Nick waiting at the church, are you?'

Nicholas! Alex was fully awake now.

'What time is it, Mel?'

'Just gone half-past nine. I daren't leave you any longer.' Melanie crossed to the window and drew back the curtains. She peered out, observing with satisfaction: 'No need to worry about whether the sun will be shining on the bride today,' and turning a teasing face, she went on: 'A good job Warren thought to ring Nick about keeping the door unlocked for you. You *were* late back!' She bustled around, picking up and putting away, tut-tutting as she hung the crumpled clover-coloured dress back on to its hanger, grumbling good-naturedly: 'It's not fair. How do you manage to look so lovely after only a few hours' sleep?'

'I don't feel lovely,' murmured Alex, stretching pleasurably. She was lying . . . she felt wonderful.

Melanie tossed Alex's robe on to the bed, opened her mouth to speak and then leaned forward, eyes widening, exclaiming:

'Alex! Where did they come from?'

Alex put a hand quickly to her throat and said self-consciously:

'Nick gave them to me last night, that's why we went back to the apartment. Aren't they nice?'

'Nice?' echoed Melanie scornfully. 'Nice? My dear girl, they're beautiful! How clever of Nick to choose pearls, they're so right for you.' She lifted a comical brow. 'I bet he didn't get those out of a Christmas cracker!' She was half-way to the door when Alex asked:

'Mel, you said that Warren rang Nick? When was that?'

'Why, last night, of course—or should I say, this morning! A whole crowd came back here for a night-cap, it was a bit hectic. They didn't leave till three and we didn't make it to bed until later than that. But it must have been around the half-twelve mark when Suzanne finally got through. We tried quite a few times, but Nick explained about dropping his cousins off first. Now then, what'll you have to drink? Orange juice? Rightio, I'll bring you up a glass and then you'd better bag the bathroom.'

As soon as the door shut Alex turned over and buried her head in the pillow, her pulses racing. Why hadn't Nick explained that the phone call had been from Warren? Why had he let her think it to be from Suzanne? An exasperated groan escaped her lips and she flung over, lying supine, all her senses alive with her thoughts. Why, why, why? So many unanswerable questions! Even now she could hardly believe what had happened between them! Admittedly, anger made one do extreme things and they had both been angry. She had thrown down the gauntlet and Nicholas had picked it up, but why? It was a most un-Nick-like situation. He never did anything on the spur of the moment. Then why had he accepted her challenge?

A blush swept over her body and she moved restlessly, closing her eyes to the harsh daylight, deliberately taking herself back to the darkened apartment.

Oh, he had been so right to suspect her innocence. Nothing had been as she had thought, least of all her own body. Nicholas had found secret places she hadn't known existed and a response that filled her with a sense of wonder. Had she surprised Nicholas too? she wondered. One word would have stopped him . . . dear heavens, he knew that and she did too . . . what a willing victim she had been!

She did breathe his name once, maybe twice, she would remember . . . not as a plea, but in capitulation. She no longer thought of anything coherently. Her body was a stranger to her, responding beyond her will, filled with unbelievable sweetness and pain, fusing into a burst of such exquisite, almost unbearable delight that she cried out and called his name.

She was gathered into his arms and cradled, breathless and shaken, then slowly her trembling ceased and she lay quiet and utterly passive.

Did she sleep? Afterwards she couldn't be sure. She remembered thinking dreamily, so this is what it will be like, sharing Nick's bed, feeling his heart beating against her back, his body curved round hers, his hand resting inert and heavily comforting along her thigh. She wondered if he slept, remembering her anger and the taunts she had thrown at him . . . remembering his gentleness, his assurance . . . dear heavens, she had learned something about herself tonight, and so had Nicholas! Frigid? She almost groaned out loud and wondered if she would ever be able to look him in the face again.

'Alex?'

So he hadn't slept.

Nicholas spoke her name softly and after a moment

raised himself on to one elbow. 'I'm sorry, my dear, but I'm afraid I shall have to take you back to Mel and Warren's. It's a pity as we're so comfortable,' gentle amusement tinged his voice, 'but unfortunately Mel will expect to see you in her guest room when she brings in the morning cup of tea and we mustn't disappoint her. And now I'll tell you why we came back here in the first place.' He moved away and there was a sense of loss with his going.

Alex half-turned, curious, and allowed her eyes to grow accustomed to the partial darkness, thinking how subtly altered everything was, how sharp awareness became. She noticed the deep hollow shadowed down the length of his spine, a ripple of curving muscle from shoulder to arm as he stretched for a box from the bedside table. With the object in his grasp Nicholas turned back, the bed dipping with the weight as he changed position, and Alex held the sheet to her with an instinctive gesture, knowing even as she did so that it was too late for maidenly modesty . . . much too late.

The sight of her now, hair streaming down her back like pale silk, the glimpse of rounded shoulder, curve of breast, was more provocative than she could possibly have realised or believed.

She said uncertainly: 'What is it?'

'Your wedding present,' he replied laconically, and surprise silenced her and she remained passive as his hands went round her neck, sweeping the fall of her hair over one shoulder while he fixed the clasp. Allowing the hair to fall back, he leaned against the headboard. 'There, let me look at you. Yes, as I thought, beautiful.' The colour rose quickly to her cheeks, for there was something in his voice that told her he was not only meaning the row of pearls now round her throat. 'Mmm . . . it seems I go in for buying you

necklaces ... the other was of jasmine, if you remember ... and came to a sorry end.'

'I ... I didn't expect a present.' Her voice was low
and husky and she cleared her throat, fingertips gently
touching the cool, smooth stones, before saying shyly:
'I don't know what to say.'

'There's no need to say anything,' he told her, eyes
half closed, voice lazy.

'I ... well, thank you.'

'Will you keep them on? I rather like the idea.'

'Yes, if you want me to.' She looked at him helplessly. The whole evening had been a bewildering confusion of emotions and she suddenly felt drained,
physically and mentally. Something of what she was
feeling must have shown in her face, because Nicholas became practical.

'We'd better get moving before search parties are
sent out.' He swung himself from the bed, reaching for
some clothing left lying on a nearby chair. He
shrugged on trousers, a sweater and canvas shoes,
raking fingers through his hair before swinging round
and looking down at her.

'I'll go and bring the car round. Can you manage?'
His eyes flicked to the clover-coloured dress lying discarded on the floor. Alex nodded, wondering if he was
remembering how easily it had come off. 'Right, I'll
be back up for you in a couple of minutes.' He made
for the door and stopped, hesitating for a moment
before saying quietly: 'Alex? You *are* feeling all right?'

When her whispered: 'Yes, thank you,' reached him
he continued to stand in the same position and at
length carried on his way. At the door he asked: 'Are
you wearing your hair up or down for the wedding?'

'I ... I haven't made up my mind,' stammered
Alex, at a loss.

'Will you wear it down? To please me?'

'Yes, of course.'

And now, lying in her own bed at Melanie and Warren's, Alex remembered the promise and the absurd pleasure it gave her to make it. Oh, you ninny, she thought with amused despair, you know you'd promise him anything!

She slid from the bed and moved slowly to the mirror. Nicholas had called her beautiful. She would need time to get used to that idea. Her eyes moved beyond her reflection to the creamy outline of the wedding dress, hanging in the background. It was a reminder. With a shiver of excitement she swept up the robe from the bed, thrust it on, and made hastily for the bathroom.

Nicholas closed the door firmly and the wedding guests' chatter was reduced to a mere background murmur.

'Oh, dear, I ought never to have had that second glass of champagne,' Alex confessed with a laugh, tossing her cream straw hat negligently on to a chair and showering the carpet with confetti. She looked round the room, assessing her feelings. She had wondered if she would feel any embarrassment, but the bright sunlight and Nicholas's matter-of-fact manner had eased her over the first few agitated seconds. 'Where did the photographer come from, Nick?'

'Ah, now that was my doing. I felt it necessary for posterity.' He opened the wardrobe door and delved inside. 'Mel says she put your travelling clothes in here—yes, here they are.' He handed them over and went on: 'The wedding cake, as you'd warned, was duly impressive.' He smiled rather cynically. 'They're all having a wonderful time in there ... they'll not even notice we've gone.'

Alex didn't reply. She was undecided what to do. Whether to take her things into the bathroom and change in there, or would that be a trifle modest, in view of only a few hours ago? Shooting a glance at Nicholas she saw that he was unbuttoning his shirt as if it were the most natural thing in the world. She gave an inward laugh. She would stay. Good heavens, she would have to get used to being married, wouldn't she?

'All three tiers.'

She looked across at him, a slight frown of incomprehension wrinkling her brow. She had managed the four tiny buttons down the side of the sleeves but was stumped by the ones at the back.

'The cake . . . all three tiers,' clarified Nicholas, and Alex grinned.

'We can give away what doesn't get eaten,' she suggested. 'Perhaps to some of your students? Wasn't it lovely of them, turning up at the church like that?'

'Yes, it was quite a surprise. You look as though you need assistance,' observed Nicholas, crossing casually over to her. 'Here, let me . . . Lord, what tiny buttons . . . not a dress to be caught in on your own, but very pretty. You're wearing your pearls, I see. There, buttons all undone . . . what terrible stuff this confetti is!' and he brushed his hand lightly across her hair and wafted a few coloured shapes into the air. 'Yes, we can throw a cake party.' He paused. 'But we'll keep one tier. The one that Mel has earmarked for . . . er . . . the christening. We don't want to offend her, do we?' His voice was bland.

Alex looked up, cheeks red.

'Oh, you wretched man! You really are infuriating sometimes.'

'Am I? But the idea isn't completely impossible, is it? Now I'm sorry to rush you, but time is ticking away and I have no desire to subject you to night driving in this country—it isn't advocated by the wise.'

After that it was quite easy to slip out of her dress and put on the simple cotton one she had chosen for the car journey. Their cases already in the boot of the Pontiac, they managed to leave without much fuss and when Bangkok was left behind Nicholas said quietly: .

'You're worrying about Ben, aren't you? I'm sure you have no need.'

Alex didn't reply. With his usual perception Nicholas had noticed her concern over her brother. Thinking back, Ben had been rather subdued for the last few days, but at their leavetaking he had been decidedly down at the mouth and she felt a pang of guilt that she had been thinking more of her own affairs during the past couple of weeks, relieved that Ben had settled in at the Carrs' with no trouble.

'It's quite a normal reaction,' Nicholas went on in his calm way. 'It's probably just hit him that he hasn't a complete claim on you now. He feels threatened. Ben'll be all right when we get back into some sort of regular routine. We'll telephone him tomorrow and have a chat.'

Alex turned impulsively: 'Oh, yes! What a kind thought. Thank you.'

Nicholas shot her a sharp glance. 'I think we should come to some agreement, Alex. I'll promise not to thank you for being a reasonable adult and you can promise the same.'

She was taken aback for a moment and then retorted lightly: 'I shall do nothing of the kind. I shall thank you just as often as I like and you'll have to put up with it.'

He smiled faintly but didn't answer. They reached Pattaya in just over three hours. Nicholas had described it as Thailand's Riviera and it was an apt description. The bay was large, blue and idyllic, dotted with small craft, water-skiers and a couple of islands. The sand was white and the shoreline was edged with palm trees. It was also full of tourists and modern hotels. As they left the skyscraper skyline behind them the coast became rougher and rockier. Round a prominence and a few miles further on Nicholas pulled into a gateway, waved at a man at the lodge-house as they went past and drove up a long drive towards the house. It was really a semi-bungalow and very charming, and at the sound of the car the door opened and an elderly Thai woman came out on to the steps to greet them, making low *wais* as they entered. While Nicholas spoke with her in Thai, Alex wandered round, enjoying the feel of the place. She stood on the verandah at the back and realised that they were closer to the sea than she had first suspected.

Hearing a footfall, she turned, leaning back against the rail. A stab of excitement shot through her, tinged very slightly with apprehension. Here she was, on her honeymoon, and the times she had been completely alone, with fear of no interruption, with Nicholas could be counted on one hand. Their row and all that had followed was there between them, remembered but not broached, and only looking at Nicholas's hands, large and strong, as they gripped the wooden rail-top as he stared out across the dipping landscape to the glimpse of sea beyond, was enough to send her nerve-ends vibrating.

'Anong is caretaker and wife of the gardener-cum-handyman and they live in the lodge-house. She speaks no English, but that shouldn't present much difficulty as I'll be around. She says there's a meal ready for us now and she'll bring eggs and milk daily and anything else we may want. I've said we'll manage for ourselves other than the evening meal. Kasem warned her of our coming, of course, and she's anxious to oblige.' He shielded his eyes against the glare of the dying sun. 'The larger island over there is Kho Larn. We'll take a boat over tomorrow, it's quite pleasant, not too spoiled by civilisation. What are you like on boats? Ever sailed before?' and he gazed down at her enquiringly.

'My dear Professor, you have no need to ask a girl brought up on the Norfolk Broads such a question! I used to spend practically all my holidays on the water.' She returned a quizzical look. 'I might even be able to teach you a thing or two.'

He gave a slow smile. 'You might at that. Good, I can leave all the hard work to you. Shall we get the things in from the car first and then eat?'

As well as the two cases there was also Nicholas's portable typewriter, which he put on a side table, and a folder bursting with papers. They were hungry, neither having eaten much of Melanie's wedding feast. Anong had provided crab and lobster with sauce, accompanied by the inevitable rice, followed by a selection of fresh fruit. Nicholas produced wine and apart from feeling as though she was a character in a stage play Alex began to enjoy herself. Afterwards they walked down the path to the sea and came to a small private cove with a jetty and a boathouse. They sat on a flat rock, watching the waves lap gently against the rise of the beach and talking in a desultory manner, mostly about the surrounding area, its people and history. Alex was interested and Nicholas informative. After a while they turned back to the house.

Although it was barely ten o'clock, Alex found herself yawning and hardly knew how to take Nicholas's comment that it had been a long day and was happy to be given the task of making a hot drink and went into the kitchen to prepare it. On her return Nicholas was sitting at the desk working. He murmured his thanks and after a moment of indecision Alex placed the cup down and said as casually as she could that she was going to bed.

Their bedroom was off the main one. She undressed, leaving the door slightly ajar so that she could still see the desk with its lamp shining down on Nicholas's bent form when she climbed into one of the single beds. That was another thing that could, or could not, be significant—twin beds! Alex thumped her pillow and switched out the bedlight. She lay on her side, her eyes gazing at the vignette-like figure at the desk. Every now and again a page would be turned and once his hand was thrust through his hair as he leaned back and stretched.

Honestly! Working on his honeymoon night! If it wasn't so mortifying it would be ludicrous. The minutes passed, and Alex found her lids drooping. A new thought hovered in the back of her mind, underpinning her pride, comforting her. Nicholas very rarely did anything without a reason ... and she juggled with the new thought and smiled sleepily. Should she stay awake or not? It seemed that nature decided for her. She woke to find the sun streaming into her eyes and the other bed crumpled, but empty. A voice said:

'I thought you were never going to wake! Come on ... we're going for a swim.' Nicholas was leaning against the doorway, in swimming trunks and a towel round his shoulders.

That set the pattern for the day. They swam, sailed and lazed. Nicholas introduced her into the art of underwater swimming and the delights of coral, fish and flora to be found on the sea-bed. Pleasantly tired, they arrived back at their cove, berthed the boat and made their way up the path towards the house.

'I wonder what Anong has left tonight,' remarked Alex, brushing dried sand from her legs and reflecting that at long last her tan was becoming quite respectable. 'I'm ravenous!'

Nicholas, coming up the verandah steps behind her, said with amusement: 'You look about fourteen with your hair like that,' and he tugged the thick plait as it hung tantalisingly down her back. Alex pulled a face and swung it over her shoulder, her hands ready to take it apart.

'It's more convenient like this . . .'

'I like it.'

Suddenly the air between them exploded with a mass of vibrations. Nicholas's smile faded and he stood looking down at her, while Alex dropped her hands to her sides, saying faintly:

'I'm glad I'm not fourteen . . .'

Anong's voice broke the silence, a sharp, staccato sentence that caused Nicholas to turn his head swiftly to where she was standing, just inside the lobby, and rap out an equally sharp question in exchange.

One look at his face told Alex something was wrong and when the exchange between Nicholas and Anong was over and Anong had glided silently away, she followed him into the house, saying anxiously:

'Nick, what is it?'

He turned and took her hands in his, saying quietly: 'Warren has phoned the Lodge. He's been trying to get hold of us all day. Ben is ill and he wants us to return as soon as we can.'

The blood drained from her face, but she replied calmly: 'What's the matter with him?' almost as if she was expecting something like this to happen.

'They're not sure. He's under observation at the moment.' Nicholas hesitated and then added: 'They're taking tests for meningitis.'

'Oh, God, no!' breathed Alex, sitting down weakly on the edge of the bed. 'It's not fatal, is it, Nick?'

'It's not diagnosed as yet, and there are drugs these days to control such things. Now then, you use the bathroom first while I start the packing,' and even as he was talking Nicholas was opening their cases and emptying drawers. 'Then we'll eat . . .'

'I couldn't eat.'

'You can try. Once we start back I'm not stopping. Off you go.'

It took them just under the hour to vacate the bungalow. They didn't talk much on the journey, Nicholas concentrating on maintaining a good speed and Alex too full of despair and guilt. She did come out of her stupor at one point to murmur:

'Nick . . . he must have been feeling ill when we left. That's why he was so quiet. Oh, why didn't he say something! He wouldn't want to be a nuisance . . .'

'A Templar trait,' commented Nicholas dryly.

'The trouble is that Ben's illnesses are never straightforward like other children's . . . and he's been doing so well lately.' With a constriction in her throat Alex turned to gaze unseeingly out of the window.

It was not meningitis—a virus, obscure but nonetheless dangerous. Three harrowing days passed by with Ben on the critically ill list. On the fifth day Nicholas brought Alex from the hospital, ruthless to her protestations, and put her to bed where she fell into an exhausted sleep. At first she was hardly aware that she was in her own room and afterwards was too proud and too apathetic to bring the matter up.

Another week saw Ben out of danger and well on the way to recovery, although very weak, and Alex began to think that perhaps there was a future to consider after all. Nicholas, it seemed, had been turning his thoughts and energy to the same subject. On the day that Ben came home, taking one look at Alex's drooping shoulders and almost translucent skin stretched tight across her cheekbones, he said abruptly:

'I had a word with the doctor at the hospital before we left. He would like Ben to be seen by the consultant who knows his case history.' He crossed and poured out a sherry, bringing the glass to her and placing it in her hand. 'Come on, drink up.'

'You're sending us back to England?'

'That's right. It's what you've wanted all along, isn't it?' he observed whimsically, pouring himself a drink.

Not without you, protested Alex silently, and sat, numb with shock and misery, while he continued matter-of-factly:

'Should you like to stay with Eleanor and Edward? I've already rung them up and they'll be delighted to have you. You like Eleanor, don't you?'

'Yes, but . . .' Alex stirred, 'I'm sure your cousins won't want to be bothered . . .'

'I gave them every opportunity to refuse.' He waited a moment, tapping his glass thoughtfully with a finger. 'Of course, England in the grip of winter isn't completely ideal, but at least you're used to it.' He took a long drink. 'Right, then, that's settled,' and switching on the desk lamp Nicholas seated himself at his typewriter and began to work.

And that was that, thought Alex. No word of when he would see us again. No comforting her and saying how much he would miss her. The ache in her throat grew until she had to escape to her room for a silent weep.

Their going was heralded with no fanfares. Nicholas drove her to the airport. The day had no business to be hot, bright and sunny. Alex, sitting silently in the back of the Pontiac, was reminded vividly of their arrival and her feelings then about Professor Nicholas Devlin. That day she had stared at the broad back with dislike and distrust. How very different were her feelings today!

The airport was all noise and bustle, but Alex was hardly aware of anything.

'Everything's arranged the other end, Alex,' Nicholas told her. 'Edward's meeting you in.' He glanced down at Ben sitting quietly on one of the lounge seats. 'Take care of your sister, Ben, and do what the doctors tell you.'

Ben stood up and put his arms round Nicholas's waist and for a few moments man and boy were silent, then Ben asked gruffly:

'When shall we see you again, Nick?'

Alex froze, waiting for the reply. Ben had asked the question she had not dared to voice.

'When I've sorted things out this end,' was the brief reply, and then: 'There's your flight number. You must go,' and disengaging the boy's arms from him he turned to Alex. 'Goodbye, Alex. Take care.'

'And you, Nick. Will you write?'

'Good God, yes,' was the rough reply. 'You must go. Now, you have your passports and tickets? Good.' He was walking her slowly towards the International

Departure checkpoint. The official waited implacably. 'Edward will look after you.' Nicholas seemed about to say something and then changed his mind, pulling her to him for a brief, hard kiss, and without waiting, turned on his heel and walked briskly out of the building.

Sitting in the plane, Alex wondered what it was he had been about to say, and gave an impatient sigh. No good speculating. They were on their way back to England. She had achieved what she had set out to do and if the process had been more traumatic and drastic than she had imagined—well, she would have to put it all down to experience. She glanced at her left hand and pensively turned the ring on her finger. A plain gold band ... and it tied her to Nicholas. Imperceptively her spirits lifted.

'Nick told me it's snowing in London,' said Ben, eyes shining. 'It says so in the papers. So we'll have a white Christmas.'

The engines began to rev and slowly the plane taxied towards the runway. With a thrust of energy it lifted into the air and Alex watched the ground leaving them, saw the coconut palms, the wooden houses, the klongs and the rice fields getting smaller and smaller. She saw the road leading from the airport into Bangkok, white and straight, dotted with tiny moving vehicles like toys.

One of those is the Pontiac, Alex reflected, and Nicholas. She wondered bleakly what his feelings were at this precise minute.

Soon they were too high up to see any more and she turned from the window, mentally leaving Thailand behind. Ahead of them lay England and an uncertain future.

CHAPTER NINE

THE Mansels lived in a house just off Sloane Square, an attractive two-storey stuccoed building, set in a row, and it combined Edward's love of old things with Eleanor's capacity for making a comfortable home. The minute she walked into the long and gracious hall Alex knew that she and Ben could be happy here, and some of her apprehension lessened slightly at the warmth of Eleanor's greeting. Edward too had welcomed them with kindly concern at the airport and as Nicholas had promised, looked after them with gratifying efficiency.

Alex was still determined to have her say, and when Ben had gone up to bed, more than ready to catch up on the seven hours they had lost in the time difference, and Edward had disappeared into his study, she tried to convey her feelings to Eleanor.

The two girls made a pleasing picture as they sat before the fire in what Eleanor called the 'snug'. This room, dominated by a huge sofa covered in chintz, also harboured an upright piano, a sewing machine and an artist's drawing board, and turned out to be Eleanor's retreat. A brindle bull-terrier, by the name of Sykes, kept them company, seeking a favourite spot between the fender and an ottoman.

Eleanor, relaxed and happy to have the chance to get to know Alex better, sat at one end of the sofa, her hazel eyes expressive, as her gaze rested thoughtfully on her guest. A tray set for coffee was on a small table at her side and some fine needlework awaited her attention on her lap.

In contrast Alex was sitting on a pouffe, her arms clasped round her knees, a slightly brooding look on her face. She was grateful for the warmth from the fire which was supplemented by a thick cardigan draped round her shoulders, borrowed from Eleanor. Her hair was loose, falling into a natural division at the back and lying forward across each shoulder, partly hiding her face which showed her inner thoughts by a small frown on her forehead.

After a few commonplace remarks Alex began shyly:

'I can't thank you and Edward enough for having us like this, Eleanor. I personally think it's a bit much, having two people foistered on to you before Christmas, but Nick insisted it was all right,' and she turned a doubtful look at Eleanor.

Eleanor smiled reassuringly. 'And so it is, honestly. These Devlins take some getting used to, I know. There's an autocratic streak in both Edward and Nicholas, inherited, so I understand, from their grandfather Devlin. My mama-in-law has it too, being a Devlin on the female side. They believe they know best and organise everybody and everything . . . it's rather annoying when more often than not they're proved right! And in this case, Nick is. There's room for you and Ben for just as long as you want it, and I'll love having you for company. As for Christmas, it will be a family affair, and you're part of the family now. It will be a good chance to meet up with the English side.'

'I've always longed to have a real family,' Alex said wistfully. 'Ben and I have been short-changed on relations and our father was away so often that it was mostly just the two of us.' She pulled a face. 'To be truthful, Eleanor, I'm scared stiff of meeting Nick's family! I mean, for him to get married like this, with hardly a word to anyone. What must they be thinking?'

'I imagine they're thrilled to bits, and you needn't worry, the Irish and American Devlins won't be here.'

'Oh, good! I need a little time before I meet Nick's parents.'

'Aunt Lydia, that's Nick's mother, has been bemoaning his single status for a long while now and has regularly produced nice American girls for him to fall in love with and he's never obliged her. She'll welcome you with open arms.'

'Well, I did have rather a nice letter from her,' confessed Alex, and Eleanor exclaimed encouragingly:

'There you are, then! You'll like Aunt Lydia, she's very attractive with amazing energy, while Uncle Pat is just the opposite, big and ugly, slow and dreamy, and a darling.' She began to pour the coffee. 'Do you think Nick will make it for Christmas?'

'I don't know, he didn't say.' It came out more forlorn than Alex intended and Eleanor, passing the coffee, said gently:

'I expect he didn't want to raise your hopes only to have them dashed down again.' She grinned mischievously. 'Don't fret, he's not going to leave a lovely new wife on her own for longer than necessary, now is he?'

Alex smiled dutifully. How she envied Eleanor, secure in her husband's love.

'You've had a rough time over the past two weeks,' commiserated Eleanor. 'Nick explained how close you and Ben are to each other and what a fragile link with life Ben had as a child. When do you take him to the hospital for the check-up?'

'Next week. I'm hoping against hope it's merely a precautionary measure.' Alex sipped her coffee pensively and went on: 'Eleanor, I'd like the chance to visit my solicitor—he's an old friend who's been good to us over the years. Do you think it would be possible for me to leave Ben with you when I go?'

'Yes, of course you can. No problem.'

'Thank you. I shall have to get our winter clothing out of store too.'

'How well do you and Ben know London?'

Alex confessed: 'Not enough to be blasé about it.'

Eleanor brightened. 'Good . . . then while you're with us we'll take you round—go to museums, art galleries and the theatre. It might help you keep from missing Nick too much.'

'It might,' echoed Alex.

She was able to journey into Norfolk with the news that Ben's tests had been optimistic. Although the more energetic forms of sport were to be omitted for a time and a second visit to the hospital was to be made in three months' time, the doctors were satisfied that no real damage had been done.

On the appointed day Alex found herself once more sitting in the waiting room of Messrs Hicks and Sloane, Solicitors, London Street, Norwich, marvelling that so much had happened since her last visit in September. Flicking over the pages of a magazine, she smiled ruefully to herself, knowing that although outwardly there seemed little difference between the Alex of September and the Alex of December, she had altered inwardly. Perhaps she had grown up? The thought made her pause and stare pensively through the window. She had even been seeing her father in a different perspective. She could never accept his emotional neglect of Ben and herself, but she had come to realise that nothing was as simple as it seemed, nothing as clear-cut as black and white, and that in the murky depths of grey there was sometimes a need for compassion. She twisted the gold band on her finger and reflected that had it not been for Charles Templar, she would never have met Nicholas. The thought warmed her. It was then that the clerk announced:

'Mr Hicks will see you now, Mrs Devlin.'

Alex smiled her thanks and sailed into James Hicks's office, wondering when her married name would cease to surprise her. The clerk closed the door behind her, sniffing appreciatively that same hint of perfume in the air and wondering why all the nice girls were snapped up by other blokes.

'Alex, my dear child, how good it is to see you!' James came round his desk, beaming, hands out in welcome. He drew her forward. 'Do sit down. Are you chilled? Pull the chair closer to the fire ... I expect our weather is a great change from the sunshine of Thailand! Well now, let me have a look at you,' and James returned to his chair, eyes twinkling. 'Whoever would have thought, four months ago, when you were berating the poor Professor for interfering in your life, that you would become his wife!' He chuckled. 'A conclusion neither of us dreamed would be possible, eh? But an extremely fortuitous one, I may say. Speaking as your legal adviser—very tidy.' He leaned across the desk, pointing a finger, with mock gravity. 'If I didn't know you better I'd have said it was a put-up job!'

Interested, Alex asked: 'How do you know it isn't, Mr Hicks?'

James rubbed an ear thoughtfully: 'Well now, Alex, for all your good sense and practical ways you're a romantic at heart, and your Professor seems to me to be a suitable contender to attract a young and attractive girl like you.'

Alex stared at him, oddly at a loss.

He nodded encouragingly. 'Yes, indeed. I was most impressed by Professor Devlin and have no qualms about you in his care.'

Alex found her voice. 'W-what do you mean, Mr Hicks? You've met ... my husband? When?' Her surprise showed on her face.

James slowly took off his spectacles, bringing out a handkerchief and beginning to clean the lenses.

'Ah ... you were unaware of his visit last month? A flying visit, in more ways than one. I believe he was due in Paris and took the opportunity of coming over to tie up some loose ends.' He replaced both the handkerchief and the spectacles and peered at her intently. 'You didn't know of this?'

'No. I knew about the Paris trip, of course, he was away three days, but that's nothing unusual, he's always being asked to speak at symposiums ...' her voice trailed as she digested this latest piece of information and she was barely aware of James continuing:

'A very clever man, your husband, Alex, very clever. A good business man, too. When do you expect him to join you?'

The pause for her answer brought Alex out of her reverie and she answered vaguely:

'I'm not quite certain yet.'

'Mm ... I was sorry to hear about Ben. How is he now?'

'Oh, much better ... the hospital's very pleased with him.'

'Good, good ... well now, the house is ready for you whenever you want it.' James opened the file in front of him and rubbed his chin, his eyes going down the pages as he turned them slowly. 'As you're here you might as well sign a couple of things that need your signature . . .'

'The house?' said Alex sharply, and James peered over his spectacles.

'On the Professor's instructions I've had a woman going in regularly and the heating's on. We don't want any burst pipes to mar your homecoming,' and he beamed complacently, before seeing the incomprehension on her face, and then his own became puzzled, and he gave the spectacles a little push with his index finger. 'Dear me, it does seem to be a day of surprises, doesn't it? Tell me, Alex, does your husband know you were coming to see me today?' He waited while she shook her head. 'I see. I assumed that he did know, and that you were aware of certain transactions that had been set in motion. Well, there's nothing we can do now. If I've betrayed a confidence it was in innocence. The Professor should have warned me that you were not to be told.'

Alex said slowly: 'Mr Hicks, are you trying to tell me that Nick . . . that my husband has bought my old home?'

'That's correct.'

'I see,' replied Alex, who didn't see at all.

'And now it won't be a surprise. What a disappointment!'

'It wasn't your fault, please don't worry about it. But I don't understand . . . you wrote to say that you'd found a buyer.'

James nodded. 'Professor Devlin instructed his solicitors to buy it from the estate, fully furnished. Everything is just as you left it.'

It was an amazing piece of information and Alex could hardly take it in. She shut her mind to the confused buzz of thoughts as to why, contenting herself with facts.

'So I could go over and stay there tonight, if I wanted to?'

'Indeed you could. I merely have to ring up the woman who goes in, to tell her you were coming.' James shook his head sadly. 'Dear, dear, the Professor will be very disappointed in me, I feel sure.'

'Now you're not to worry, Mr Hicks. My husband is rather over-fond of secrets and it's his own fault if they sometimes backfire on him.' Alex rummaged in her bag for her pen. 'What is it you want me to sign?'

By the time Alex left him, James Hicks had allowed his ruffled feelings to be soothed and she took a bus to her home and entered it with a full heart. Outwardly it hadn't much to commend it, being of old red brick, solidly square and fairly private in a walled garden which backed on to a golf course. But she had hated it having to be sold, had always loved it, choosing to remember the first eight happy years to sustain her through the lonely latter ones.

As she trailed through all the rooms she acknowledged that 'the woman', whoever she was, was competent. The place seemed as fresh and clean as when they had left. The telephone was disconnected, so she walked down the familiar road to a callbox and spoke to Eleanor, and then to Ben, to say she was staying over, then made her way back. The snow was thicker on the ground here than in London, and crunched satisfyingly under foot. She was glad to get into the warm house. Taking her hands from the pockets of her coat, she brought out also the first letter she had ever had from Nicholas.

The ink was black and the writing was large and symmetrical. It was a pleasant, interesting letter, but not what she wanted. Why had he bought the house?

And before proposing marriage to her! She returned to London the next day and decided to keep the news of the house to herself for the time being.

Christmas came and went, and any hope that Nicholas would join them faded with a telephone call—wildly expensive, according to Eleanor—on Christmas Day. He sounded in good spirits. He was ringing from Mel and Warren's where he was spending the day, and the sound of his voice filled Alex with a desperate longing.

Fifteen minutes to the New Year found the Mansel house full of people, noisy with celebrating the advent of a new decade. Alex caught Eleanor's eye, saw a rather anxious look directed at herself and smiled reassuringly. She was sitting alone at the moment and quite happy to do so, but it was like Eleanor to worry about her. She had suddenly needed a respite from socialising, had begun to weary giving the same explanations about herself, each time making the distance between herself and Nicholas longer. She sipped her drink thoughtfully and wondered why a new year should matter so much, coming to the conclusion that human nature being what it was she supposed it heralded renewed hope and optimism. She gave a wry smile, thinking that her own future needed both.

An argument arose about the correct time and the television set was switched on and an announcer's voice was excitedly proclaiming that Big Ben would soon be sounding the first strokes of midnight. The picture showed the crowds waving and cheering as they waited, packed into Trafalgar Square, flags waving. Edward came over to her, refilling her glass in readiness for the toast. He smiled, asked if she was all right, and moved on.

Another year nearly over, thought Alex, and wondered what the new one held for her.

Every man is responsible for his own destiny.

The words came to her suddenly, exploding in her head, and as suddenly she made a decision. She would write to Nicholas and tell him everything—her hopes, her fears and her love. Then it would be up to him. She felt a great burden lift and gave a satisfied sigh. No matter what the outcome was it would be better than this state of limbo. She stood up and rejoined the party, allowing herself to be drawn into the laughing, jovial, friendly crowd, ready to accept other people's happiness.

One, two, three . . . the numbers were chanted in time with the sound of Big Ben's chimes . . . eleven, twelve! Happy New Year! Should auld acquaintance be forgot . . . Hands were joined, voices sang out . . . For the sake of Auld Lang Syne!

Hugs and kisses were exchanged. Alex found herself grabbed by perfect strangers, everyone benevolent and filled with bonhomie.

'Happy New Year, Alex,' said Edward, giving her a friendly kiss, his eyes smiling. Before she could reply, arms twirled her round and laughingly, she began:

'Happy New . . .' and the words died.

'Happy New Year, Alex,' said Nicholas, looking huge in a thick sheepskin jacket, snowflakes still glistening on his hair. He kissed her, long and thoroughly. A cheer went up and, breathless and red-cheeked, Alex was released.

A voice called: 'A drink for the first-footer!' and Nicholas was dragged away and handed a glass, friends coming up to shake his hand or kiss him, depending on their sex, and all the time their eyes kept meeting. What showed on Alex's face she had no way of telling . . . on Nicholas's was an expression of bland self-satisfaction.

Wretched, wretched man! He knew—she could tell. Somehow she had given herself away.

Before she could go any further with this line of thought Alex was whirled round and wished a hearty New Year greeting by a fair-haired, bearded man she vaguely recognised. He kissed her with relish, saying cheerily:

'Who's the first-footer, do you know?'

A silly, ridiculous bubble of happiness was lurking deep inside Alex, ready to burst, but she wasn't ready to let that happen yet. Not until she was sure.

'My husband,' she replied demurely, and laughed outright at her partner's mock-horrified reaction.

'Oh, my Lord! The man's enormous and he looks as though he packs a healthy punch too. Help! He's coming over,' and bowing with a theatrical flourish he backed away, laughing.

But Nicholas was making for the door and it was Eleanor who came over.

'Alex, my dear, I know you must be longing to have Nick to yourself. Don't bother about us,' and giving her a fierce hug she pushed Alex into the hall. 'He's in Edward's study.'

Two large cases stood by the bottom of the stairs, a ranger hat hung on the hat stand and the sheepskin coat was flung over the end of the banister.

With a thumping heart Alex made her way down the hall and pushed open the door to Edward's study. Nicholas was standing by the fire, one arm resting along the mantelpiece, gazing downwards. He looked up at her entrance and straightened, a quizzical look on his face.

'Hullo, Alex. Pleased to see me?'

'Yes, of course . . . and surprised.' She moved forward, but still keeping a distance between them, and allowed her eyes to take their fill, trying for calmness. Mindful of the English weather he was wearing a thick navy fisherman-type jersey, and grey corded pants. The outfit made him seem bigger and more over-powering than ever. Alex was determined to be composed.

His brows shot up. 'Surprised?' His eyes were clear and candid, but there was the hint of an upward tilt to his mouth. He was an infuriating man and she was going to give him a run for his money.

'Why, yes, you didn't say anything about coming over when you telephoned at Christmas.' Her voice was beautifully cool.

'There seemed no point until I was certain,' he came back smoothly. 'And when I do arrive, what do I find? My wife being kissed by a devil-may-care actor!'

'It's a shame, but one never knows who one can trust these days,' agreed Alex, all sympathy, and was rewarded by the beginning of a smile. 'Are you hungry? Can I get you anything?'

The smile broadened. She had forgotten how white his teeth were against the tan, and how craggy his face was, how infinitely dear.

'No, you must surely have forgotten how they feed you on airlines, although your concern is very pleasant.' He placed his glass carefully on the mantelpiece and said mildly: 'Don't I get a wifely kiss, Alex?' and his eyes were no longer clear or candid, but were half-closed and speculative.

Damn his eyes, thought Alex weakly, it's just not fair! She held out a little longer, lifting a disdainful shoulder.

'To be truthful, Nick, I don't feel particularly wifely at the moment. In fact, it's taking me all my time to feel I'm really married.' She glanced sideways at him beneath lowered lashes. How clever of her to be wearing her clover-coloured dress. Was it bringing back memories for him too? she wondered. She trembled slightly. Challenging Nicholas had never been a particularly clever thing to do in the past. What if she was wrong? What if her hopes and dreams were merely wishful thinking?

There was a distinctly dangerous gleam in his eyes at this moment and his voice was silky as he answered her.

'Well now, we shall have to do something about that, shan't we?' He crossed to a small holdall lying on the floor and yanked open the zip, bringing from its depths a long, thin box. He turned and clicked it open, lifting the pearls between two fingers. 'You left your pearls behind, Alex,' he scolded gently. 'On purpose, I wonder? Perhaps I can exchange them for that wifely kiss I asked for.' He smiled lazily. 'Is that a fair enough bargain?'

She was having difficulty breathing as he approached, her heart seemed to be thumping somewhere in her throat. Wordlessly she turned her back, sweeping her hair forward while he lay the pearls against her skin, his fingers brushing the back of her neck, sending a shiver down her spine. Moving slowly round again, she let her hair fall and standing on tiptoes placed her hands, palm downwards against his chest, feeling the wool rough, his body hard to her touch. Lifting her face, she rested her lips gently against his own, her eyes open, fixed on his.

She took a pace back and regarded him gravely. 'Was that suitable to the terms of our contract?'

He stood, hands on hips, towering over her. His lips pulled into a derisive smile and he drawled: 'Oh, yes, coming well within the bounds of admiration, companionship and respect, as befitting Professor Devlin—the poor fool—and the tantalisingly beautiful Miss Templar.' He jutted his jaw, his eyes gleaming. 'And now will you forget all that damned nonsense, my very dear and infinitely sweet Alexandra Jane?' His voice was a caress and her own came out uneven and breathless, the colour flooding her cheeks, her ears pounding.

'You know, don't you, how I feel about you?'

'Only hoped, you adorable creature! Come here, I won't wait any longer! You must tell me how you feel!' and sweeping her to him Nicholas kissed her urgently. 'Don't you realise, woman, that I'm mad about you? That you're indispensable to me? That I'm no use to man nor beast without you?' His voice was husky, filled with amused anguish as his lips travelled possessively, touching her face, caressing her neck, hollow of throat, back again to her tremulous mouth, kissing her between sentences.

'Oh no ... how could I know?' protested Alex weakly, her senses a tumult, the blood rushing through her veins, making her feel alive again for the first time since the eve of their wedding, his words filling her with joy.

He groaned deeply. 'Damn it all, Alex, surely I showed you?'

The laughter bubbled out. Holding back her head, she murmured throatily: 'With such an expert lover, how could I possibly know I was getting star treatment?' and her hands came up to thrust fingers through his hair, intermingling round the back of his head. Her eyes laughed up at him as she pulled his mouth down, and then the laughter died as the initiative was taken from her, and her lips parted be-

neath his. Sensuous tremors ran through her as his
hands stroked and moved, holding her possessively,
re-learning curve of shoulder, hollow of back, mound
of hip and thigh.

'Oh, Nick, I've missed you so,' she whispered, and
he gave a jubilant laugh and tightened his hold.

'Good. I wanted you to.' He swept her up into his
arms and strode across the room, reaching out to open
the door.

'Nick! What about Eleanor and Edward?' she protested weakly, as he carried her inexorably up the
stairs.

He grinned wickedly. 'If they expected to see either
of us again tonight I've grossly underrated their sen-
sibilities.' He stopped to kiss her masterfully. 'Which
room, woman?' and when she laughingly pointed, he
marched along the landing, pushing the door open.
Alex whispered teasingly:

'It's a twin-bedded room,' and Nicholas came back
solemnly:

'Then we'll save on the laundry bill. Thank God the
place is centrally heated. After temperatures in the
eighties your country takes some adjusting to, my
love,' and he kicked the door shut with his foot. He
stood looking down for a moment into her face, his
own tender, then setting her gently on her feet, remarked casually: 'I seem to remember that this dress
comes off quite easily,' and his brow quirked.

Alex eased her shoulder tentatively, thinking with
amusement that when it came to sharing a single bed
with Nicholas he was bound to come out the winner
by sheer size alone. She was completely enveloped and
wondered whether she dared move, not wanting to
waken him. She flexed a leg carefully. Ah, that was

better. She lay for a while, listening to his steady breathing, a smile on her face. Lovely, lovely New Year. She stirred again, compelled to move, gently, stealthily, until suddenly she knew he was awake and watching her.

'Oh, you brute,' she murmured against his chest. 'How do you expect me to sleep with a great big bear like you hogging all the bed?' and she stretched pleasurably, easing her aching muscles, then allowing her body to relax against him again.

'That's the main idea, my love,' came the lazy reply, and then: 'Are you too cramped?'

'No . . . don't leave me. My leg was going to sleep.'

'I have no intention of leaving you. Which leg? This one?' and Nicholas rubbed it briskly for a few seconds. 'Is that better?' and Alex gave a contented sigh.

'Mm . . . much better.' She lay, eyes closed and said presently: 'Nicholas.'

'Yes?'

'I went to see Mr Hicks last week.' Silence.

'Did you now?'

'Uhuh . . . Why did you buy the house, Nick?'

'Why do you think?' His voice was a lazy tease and she lifted her head from his shoulder and searched his face.

'Are we going to live there? Really?'

'Yes, really!' he mocked, and impulsively she responded:

'Oh, Nick, how good you are!'

'That's not always been your opinion,' he observed dryly. 'There was a time when I was the man you loved to hate.'

Alex laughed softly and buried her face into his chest. 'It took some doing, but I did manage to for a while.' She hesitated and went on shyly: 'Why did you ask me to marry you, Nick?'

'Because I loved you.' He smoothed the hair from her face and kissed just above her ear. 'I kept it businesslike and practical . . . I didn't want to frighten you away.'

'And did you really think I would marry you for Ben's sake?' she persisted gently, and Nicholas gave a short laugh.

'Oh, yes, it seemed quite in keeping with your character and what I'd observed for myself. You were such a prickly little thing, flaring up like a mother cat over her kitten. Of course, I knew that you were beginning to see me in a more kindly light . . . which was a small comfort . . . and I'd had some rather interesting news from Ben too.'

Alex lifted her head, puzzled, and Nicholas went on:

'You remember when he ran away? Lord, what a panic we were in! All Suzanne's fault, the silly woman. She said something to him about you going back to England and really upset him. He was in quite a state when I found him and sobbed out that now you were talking of leaving him with me. That was a surprise, I can tell you. I began to think that perhaps I might stand a chance, hence the cool, practical marriage proposal. I didn't expect you to agree so quickly and seem so damned cool and practical yourself . . .'

Alex groaned a laugh. 'If you only knew!'

'If we both had only known!' quipped Nicholas. 'Anyway, I went ahead with the plans at full speed—I wanted you tied to me, you see, in case you changed your mind before I could make you love me, but I couldn't resist the few crumbs I could legitimately take from your table. Every time I touched you . . .' he stopped short and smiled ruefully. 'Well, I know now why you resisted, but at the time it was hell.'

Alex murmured softly: 'And then Eleanor and Edward arrived.'

'Yes. Eleanor and Edward arrived.' Nicholas was silent for a moment and when he began to speak again his voice was low. 'You were so right about that night. I was damnably jealous of Edward and I had cold feet ... for both of us. Suppose I was wrong? Suppose I couldn't make you love me and you were really marrying me completely for Ben's sake? It was a hell of a risk for both of us, and the sight of Eleanor and Edward together bulldozed my confidence. Until ...' He peered down at her, a wicked gleam in his eyes.

'Until I offered myself to you,' supplied Alex demurely, and she snuggled closer. 'How angry we were that night!'

Nicholas laughed complacently. 'When I found out what was making you so angry—Suzanne—why, I stopped being angry. No one who was cold and unfeeling would be jealous ...'

'Don't you try and tell me ...!'

His fingers touched her lips, stilling the words. 'I won't try and tell you anything, my love, except that she hadn't a hope in hell's chance with me, ever. It was a pretty mean trick letting you think different, but it got results, didn't it?'

Alex bit his finger gently, trying to hide her delight. 'Mmm ... it was also a pretty mean trick making an honest woman of me and then ignoring me on my wedding night! Wretched man! Brute!' The word was an endearment. 'I know why you did it, though.'

'Oh? Do you now?'

'Yes, Professor dear, I do. You were showing me that love can be a gift or a payment and that just because you'd married me it didn't mean you would demand payment.' She slanted him a glance. 'I ... I was beginning to think that perhaps you were coming to care for me a little ... and then you sent me away without saying a word.'

'I know. I still wasn't sure you loved me. Eleanor, bless her, blasted into me on the telephone and told me I was a fool and when was I coming over to put you out of your misery! Have I done that, Alex?'

There was no need for her to reply. After a while Nicholas said: 'When shall we go to Norwich?'

'Let's go soon, Nick!'

They stared at each other and burst out laughing. Alex shook her head in protest.

'Nick, we can't! Can we?'

'Why not? The house is ready. It won't take you long to pack up yours and Ben's cases ...'

'They're already packed,' she broke in sheepishly. 'I was going home tomorrow ...'

He grinned. 'So what's in a day?' He lifted his wrist and looked at his watch. 'We'll eat a hearty breakfast and be off. I've got a car, Edward organised it for me, so there's nothing to stop us.'

The car turned out to be a Chevrolet, large and yellow, with left-hand steering. Ben was tremendously excited when he saw it, but Alex covered her eyes and groaned loudly.

'Is this it?' she demanded at last, and Nicholas grinned, opening the passenger door and bowing her in. She did so, laughing. He joined her the other side and she exclaimed: 'Oh, Nick, how could you! Can you imagine what a reaction this will cause in Norfolk? And it must gobble up petrol!'

'It is a bit thirsty,' conceded Nicholas, showing her how to fasten the seat belt. 'A man has to have something to take his mind off the shackles of matrimony,' he told her, giving her a hard, brief kiss.

'It's an American car, Nick?' asked Ben from the back, his voice awed.

'Correct, my lad.'

'That's right, Ben,' murmured Alex, giving her husband an indulgent side glance. 'It's a big, bossy Yank—like its owner,' and then she added resignedly: 'It'll never fit in the garage!'

The snow had turned to slush and was being washed away by a steady downpour of rain. As the windscreen wipers swished back and forth Alex was reminded of Singapore and thought that both she and Nicholas had come a long way since then. She still couldn't believe that he loved her, couldn't believe her luck. Feeling her eyes upon him, Nicholas turned to smile, taking her hand and giving it a squeeze before resuming his grip on the steering wheel.

They had a late lunch in Cambridge, the Chevrolet proving of great interest to passers-by, and set off again, the rain continuing to fall steadily. Thetford, Attleborough and Wymondham were soon behind them and then they hit the Norwich ring-road, branching off on the eastern side towards the Broads.

Talk in the car had almost ceased, Ben had dropped off to sleep, Alex was daydreaming and Nicholas concentrating on the narrow roads. Barely four o'clock, it was still necessary for car lights to be used, and rounding a corner Nicholas suddenly gave an exclamation, slammed on the brakes and then hit the water, sending a huge wave either side of the car. The engine died. There was silence and then Nicholas hit the steering wheel with his fist in exasperation.

'Would you believe it? The road's flooded!'

Alex peered out, hearing the rain beating down on the Chevrolet's roof and windows. 'So it is! Goodness, the River Bure must have overflowed with all the snow and rain!' and she turned a dismayed face to Nicholas.

'This is where we came in, if I remember rightly,' he stated with grim humour, trying the engine to no avail, and Alex laughed and pulled a wry face.

'No twelve-foot drains here, darling,' she soothed. 'Nick, I am sorry. I oughtn't to have brought us the country way . . .'

'There's something coming up behind,' observed Nicholas, opening his door and looking back along the lane. 'We're in luck, Alex, it's a tractor,' and he stepped out into the water, cursing under his breath as it struck cold and wet, banging the door shut behind him.

Ben, who was now awake, peered out of the back window and said excitedly:

'It's Mr Bletchley, from Upton Farm.'

Mr Bletchley it was, most happy to tow young Alex Templar and her new husband out of the floods, even though it was raining cats and dogs. He was the possessor of a sou'wester and waterproof cape, so the weather worried him not at all. Alex, who held the torch while they fixed the tow rope, and Nicholas, inadequately dressed, suffered more.

An hour later they were swinging out of Upton Farm gates, having partaken of a cup of tea in Mrs Bletchley's kitchen while the Chevrolet's ignition was dried out, and after a couple of miles Alex began to giggle. She leaned across and wiped a trickle of water coursing down Nicholas's cheek with her handkerchief.

'Just what are you laughing about?' he asked in mock anger, and she burst out laughing.

'Nick, if you could only see yourself! I don't suppose I look much better. We do seem to have an affinity to floods, don't we?'

'So it would seem, Naiad.' He was silent for a moment and then said whimsically: 'I was going to deliver you to your brother and find out where you were staying ... that night in Singapore, I mean.'

'Were you, Nick?' replied Alex softly. 'I think I fell a little in love with you that night. It was only natural, I suppose.'

'Of course,' said Nicholas smugly. 'Do we turn right here?'

'Oh, yes ... look, Ben, we're nearly home.' And then: 'The outside light's on ... good old Mr Hicks.'

Nicholas drove up the short driveway and pulled to a halt outside the front door porch. The rain was beating down inexorably and the lantern swung in the wind sending the light shining eerily round the surrounding shrubbery.

'Key?' Nicholas asked, and Alex searched in her handbag and found it. 'Right, I'll open the front door and come back for Ben. We might as well have one member of the family remaining dry.'

As he left them Alex responded to his words with a warm glow. She and Ben were now Nicholas's family. He had just said so. Ben enjoyed the piggyback his guardian gave him to the house, but when Nicholas returned Alex was already out, feeling she was wet enough. They stood looking at each other in the pouring rain and began to laugh, slowly and quietly at first, building up into whoops of laughter as they clung to each other.

'The neighbours will think we're mad,' gasped Alex as Nicholas pulled her to him.

'And they'd be right ... but who cares?' He kissed her hard and lifted her into his arms, ignoring her protests. 'Well, Alexandra Jane Devlin, shall we cross the threshold together?'

She smiled into his grey eyes and said simply: 'Yes, please, Professor,' and felt his arms tighten. 'I don't mind where we go, so long as we go together.'

'Good. That's a deal,' said Nicholas.

'What are you doing?'

They turned their heads to the lighted doorway to see Ben, back from his tour of the house, standing in the hall looking out.

'Aren't you coming in? I'm famished!'

'Yes, we're coming.' replied Nicholas, smiling at Alex, as he carried her into the house and closed the door behind them.